Mary Putnam Jacobi

Common Sense

Applied to Woman Suffrage

Mary Putnam Jacobi

Common Sense
Applied to Woman Suffrage

ISBN/EAN: 9783337418717

Printed in Europe, USA, Canada, Australia, Japan

Cover: Foto ©Andreas Hilbeck / pixelio.de

More available books at **www.hansebooks.com**

"COMMON SENSE"

APPLIED TO

WOMAN SUFFRAGE

A STATEMENT OF THE REASONS WHICH JUSTIFY THE DEMAND
TO EXTEND THE SUFFRAGE TO WOMEN, WITH CON-
SIDERATION OF THE ARGUMENTS AGAINST SUCH
ENFRANCHISEMENT, AND WITH SPECIAL
REFERENCE TO THE ISSUES PRE-
SENTED TO THE NEW YORK
STATE CONVENTION
OF 1894

BY

MARY PUTNAM-JACOBI, M.D.

G. P. PUTNAM'S SONS

NEW YORK   LONDON
27 W. Twenty-third Street   24 Bedford Street, Strand
The Knickerbocker Press
1894

CONTENTS.

iii

"COMMON SENSE" APPLIED TO WOMAN SUFFRAGE.

" Who the author of this Production is, is wholly unnecessary to the Public, as the object for attention is the Doctrine *itself*, not the man. Yet it may not be unnecessary to say,—That he is unconnected with any party, and under no sort of Influence, public or private, but the influence of reason and principle."—*Common Sense*, Addressed to the Inhabitants of America, January 10, 1776.

" Not he is great who alters matter, but he who alters my state of mind."—EMERSON, The American scholar.   Phi Beta Kappa oration.

THE celebrated pamphlet from which—not without audacity—we have borrowed our title-page, is said to have been an important factor in the formation of the public opinion,* which six months later, decided to risk the Revolutionary War. To-day is also a moment for the formation of a public opinion,—opinion on a question not less momentous, upon issues even more far-reaching than those involved in the famous quarrel of our ancestors with their mother country.

* " This pamphlet, whose effect has never been equalled in literary history."—*Works of Thomas Paine*, Moncure Conway.

1

"The sun never shined on a cause of greater worth. 'T is not the affair of a city, a country, a province, or a kingdom, but of a continent of at least the eighth part of the habitable globe. 'T is not the concern of a day, a year, or an age ; posterity are virtually involved in the contest, and will be more or less affected even to the end of time, by the proceedings now."

"A situation similar to the present hath not happened since the days of Noah until now." *

To-day, also, a change is proposed, not as a despairing revolt against a really intolerable oppression, or physical cruelty, but against grievances only appreciable by those who have already attained a fair measure of independence. To-day, also, the demand for a share in the sovereignty of the State is the expression, on the part of those demanding, of a higher degree of development than had previously been attained, and of an imperious impulse towards still further expansion, power, and autonomy.

"Small islands not capable of protecting themselves are the proper objects for government to take under their care, but there is something absurd in supposing a continent to be perpetually governed by an island. In no instance has nature made the satellite larger than the primary planet." †

* *Common Sense*, pp. 84, 118.   † *Common Sense*, p. 92.

To-day, also, the protest, the declaration of independence, does not receive the unanimous support of the classes on whose behalf it is made. There are Tories in the midst, and plausible reasons are advanced even by women, against the demand made for them, to be allowed to "take, among the powers of the earth, the separate and equal place to which the laws of Nature and of Nature's God entitle them."

"Interested men who are not to be trusted, weak men who cannot see, prejudiced men who will not see, and a certain set of moderate men who think better of the European world than it deserves, are those who espouse the doctrine of reconciliation." *

And to-day, as in 1776, the demand to emerge into political individuality, from a condition of political non-existence,—the demand to become recognized factors in the political life of the State, implies, and also forebodes changes in the social status of those demanding, which is of far more consequence than any of the special reasons which may be urged in support of the demand.

"The birthday of a new world is at hand, and a race of men, perhaps as numerous as all Europe contains, are

* *Common Sense*, p. 90.

to receive their portion of freedom from the events of a few months. The reflection is awful,—and in this point of view how trifling, how ridiculous do the little paltry cavillings of a few weak and interested men appear, when weighed against the business of a world." *

The modern position of women was inaugurated by the Revolution of 1848. The Revolution of 1688 overthrew the doctrine of the divine right of kings. The Revolution of 1793 dissolved the doctrine of the necessary and lawful supremacy of social classes. The Revolution of 1848 asserted the human rights of the individual. In France the masses obtained equality before the law in 1793; they did not obtain political equality for men until 1848. In Germany, the political equality, temporarily gained, was lost in the reaction, to be reacquired later, so far as universal suffrage was concerned, with the establishment of the German Empire.

In England, the great Reform Bill of 1832, had preceded '48, and softened its shock,† which expended itself in the Chartist movement, and the monster petition to Parliament. Crossing the Atlantic, the ebbing wave of the Revolu-

* *Common Sense*, p. 118.

† Or perhaps precipitated, by the extensive disfranchisements of the poorer classes, which the Bill, though reforming " rotten " boroughs, brought about.

tion found the political rights of men already fairly secured ; the restrictions remaining upon universal manhood suffrage slight : the force of the wave expended itself upon the legal, social, and political disabilities of women.

The way had been prepared for this special direction of the Revolutionary movement, in a remarkable manner. Already had begun the intensification of the anti-slavery movement, which had been initiated by the Quaker petition framed immediately after the adoption of the Constitution ; and the New England Anti-Slavery Society had been formed in 1832. Two women, Lucretia Mott and Esther Moore, were among the founders of this society, and in 1840 were sent as delegates to an anti-slavery convention in England. With these, went Elizabeth Cady Stanton, whose husband was also a delegate. But the convention refused to receive the female delegates, sent in good faith by the American members, on the ground that all public function for women was " in defiance of God's ordination."

Whereupon William Lloyd Garrison refused to take any part in the proceedings, and withdrew to a seat in the galleries, where he remained during the entire twelve days of the session. This was not the least service rendered by this heroic man to the cause of consistency and equal rights!

The abolitionists in America felt more rebuked by the action of their English brethren, than fortified by Garrison's protest against English discourtesy. They presently forbade women to speak on their platforms, and Lucy Stone was among the first to be so excluded. They followed, but only for a few years, the example of the churches, and secured the assistance of women in work, as on the underground railroad, while trying to exclude them from publicity, responsibility, or honor. However, after a few years this artificial division of labor broke down; women did speak for the slave in public, but in so doing found arrayed against themselves, not only England, but the American church. The church was already arrayed against abolitionism in the interests of "harmony." * The "indecent" publicity of the women abolitionists was a subordinate incident, but it would serve as a handle for attack, and was wielded manfully. The abolitionists were declared to have set aside the laws of God

---

* "O harmony!" will exclaim some future Madame Roland; "how many hypocrisies have been perpetrated in thy name!"

when they allowed women to speak in public; and by a pastoral letter, the Congregational churches of Massachusetts were directed to defend themselves against heresy, by closing their doors against the innovators. The Methodists denounced the Garrisonian societies as " no-government, no-sabbath, no-church, no-bible, no-marriage, women's rights societies."

Yet at the anti-slavery meetings no discussion had ever taken place in regard to women; every one was entirely absorbed in the cause of the slave. However, here, as often, it happened that the instinct of the conservative saw farther than the conscious intention of the radical. The practical demonstration of the capacity of women to engage effectively, nobly, publicly, in such a great national enterprise as that then initiated for the abolition of slavery, constituted a far more powerful argument for the general emancipation of the sex than the most elaborate philosophical dissertation could have been.

However, so single-minded were these women, so absorbed in the emancipation of the slave from bondage, that they would probably not have thought of their own emancipation from restrictions, had it not been for the unexpectedly unkind and ungenerous treatment which they received at the hands of their friends. For the abolitionists again tried to purge themselves of the contempt cast upon them by the churches by submitting to the one criticism which did not involve the men of their party, and for two years the voices of women were silenced.*

But who can silence the voice of woman when she is determined to speak, and still less when she really has something to say? It is a circumstance at once dramatic, piquant, and almost comical, that the immediate motive for the call to the first Woman's Rights Convention was not the pressure of the numerous personal, legal, and social disabilities which then weighed so heavily upon women, but prohibition to speak, and to speak on behalf of the slave. This fact at least furnished the electric spark which fused together all the many tendencies which had been long smouldering in

---

* In the same way the Methodists had forbidden the continuance of the female preachers, at first allowed. Arguments may be drawn for the discouragement of female oratory, far more plausible than those based on a supposed but unrecorded " ordinance of God." Yet if women's orations have often been disfigured by hysteric excitability, or shallow sentimentality, or ignorant verbosity, the names of Lucy Stone, Lucretia Mott, Mrs. Stanton, Mrs. Howe, and Mrs Livermore, to mention no others, suffice to prove that the woman orator can exist.

secret. Perhaps they did not themselves know that it was because the ideas of 1848 were in the air,—were making the circuit of the globe, —because on the eastern shore of the Atlantic there had been a revolution in February and an insurrection in June; that in July, on the western side, in New York State, at Seneca Falls, Lucretia Mott, Elizabeth Cady Stanton, and Susan B. Anthony called together the first Woman's Rights Convention. The assertion is not bombastic that there also was " fired a shot heard round the world ! "

" We fully believed," observed Antoinette Blackwell the other day, " so soon as we saw that woman's suffrage was right, every one would soon see the same thing, and that in a year or two, at farthest, it would be granted."

With such innocence and naïveté did these single-hearted women come into collision with the entire organized system of traditions, beliefs, prejudices, convictions, habits, laws, and customs which had hitherto existed from the beginning of history down to the year of grace, 1848! No wonder the shock was great! The marvel is that in it everything was not shivered to splinters !

History had ceased to exist for that American

decade; for to all the living issues of the day, history, like the Church and the State, seemed to those in the van, to be either irrelevant or hostile. To this very day the survivors of that group of pioneer women retain an abstract way of stating their claim which, to modern ears, sounds somewhat archaic. When we compare the transparent simplicity of the arguments of that time, with the painful erudition, the elaborate research which European scholars have accumulated on the subject of the Rights of Women,* we seem to be comparing an out-line drawing of Flaxman's, with a thickly de-tailed painting of Rubens. I even, in imagina-tion, am led to contrast the gentle savages of Hispaniola dancing in the garb of Eden on the sea-shore, where had just landed, in doublet and ruff, the representatives of Spanish gran-dees.

To-day a fine and certainly widely diffused scorn prevails for doctrines of abstract Rights and of claims based on them. Yet how can a demand for Rights ever be formulated except abstractly ? When did such a demand ever seem " practical " or "useful " to the class mo-

---

* See, for instance, Laboulaye's Memoir with this title, recom-pensed by the French Academy in 1842.

nopolizing the Rights demanded ? What human
conception is more abstract, more finely abstract,
than that of Rights?) What conception more
august, more mysterious in the power which it
presently discloses to subdue the most brutal
forces, to chain the most material oppositions, to
trample under foot the most obvious utilities ?
No matter what its philosophic basis, or what
its historic evolution, the conception of Right
at any given time dominates, quite apart from
either metaphysics or history. No one dares to
deny it, for the gist of every issue and the
heart of every conflict is the question : " On
which side does the Right lie, which both
sides claim ? "

In 1848 the party had arisen, small as a grain
of mustard seed, which had acquired a profound distrust of all the authoritative dictates
of a society that was then engaged in defending
the lawfulness of American slavery. If this
were the authorized conception of Rights, then
the judgment of society was steeped in wrong,
and an appeal must be carried to a higher court.
The horrible mess of sophistry, cant, and mean-
ness with which was being sustained the national argument for slavery, inevitably loosened
confidence in public opinion. One almost uni-

versal dictum was certainly wrong : there was
an almost indefinite possibility that any other
might be untrue.

The woman's movement began, therefore,
with that for the slave, in one common fact,—
a suddenly awakened but profound distrust of
all authority.

Soon further analogies appeared. To both
women and negroes were forbidden liberty of
action, except under such conditions as some
one else should impose. To both comfort was
possible, on condition of peaceful submission to
such restrictions as another's will should deem
best. The restrictions were extremely narrow
for the slave, while a much wider range was accorded the woman ; but to neither was complete
self-determination permitted. All negroes and
all white women differed from white men, in
that their liberties were restrained by a greater
number of considerations than the one imposed
on men,—that, namely of not violating the liberty of any one else. In this fundamental particular, therefore, the case of the women and the
negroes was identical,—it was the details only
which differed. The immense differences in
regard to practical details could not change the
identity of the fundamental facts.

Then the question arose :—Ah ! mighty is the age which asks a question !—By what right did those who had the power impose restrictions on those who had not? Who authorized them? The women's credentials had been refused. Who had given their credentials to those refus- ing? Why should the whole moral and physi- cal force of society be enlisted to support their monstrous claim? Why should Federal troops be employed to chase runaway slaves in the streets of Boston? Why should clergymen in the pulpit be engaged to prescribe, with all the thunders of Sinai, what the free white women of America should or should not do?

It is not a piece of turgid rhetoric which asso- ciates these two piercing questions together. It is a simple historic fact that they were so asso- ciated; that they came to the front together; that the demand of women for political rights was made because their personal liberty had been assailed—assailed at the moment that they had begun to work to secure the personal liberty of the slave. And in the shock of the unex· pected assault, they had become suddenly aware within what narrow bounds their own personal liberties were really expected to maintain them· selves.

And so the definite, the final conflict began. The protest against political inequality, uttered at Seneca Falls, fell back from the buttressed fortress of existing political institutions like a ball of feathers from a wall of adamant. Then the women began a flank movement. They attacked the laws, they pressed into industries, they demanded education. Even before the Woman's Rights Convention, Mrs. Stanton had been working to secure independent property rights for married women, and after seven years' struggle the end was attained. Then began a second struggle for personal rights in contracts and business, and these also were secured after a steady fight of twelve years. " They tell us sometimes," said Mrs. Stanton at the great mass-meeting in New York on the 7th of May, " that if we had only kept quiet, all these desirable things would have come about of themselves. I am reminded of the Greek clown who, having seen an archer bring down a flying bird, remarked, sagely : ' You might have saved your arrow, for the bird would anyway have been killed by the fall.' "

Since 1848 such changes have been effected in the personal, industrial, legal, and educational status of women, the revolution in public opin-

ion about women has been so enormous, that
there is no century, nor five nor ten centuries
of all preceding European history, which can
compare with it. Innumerable claims have been
satisfied which forty-six years ago were absolutely disallowed. Innumerable arguments,
apparently as irrefutable as those of the English
bucolics frightened by Stephenson's locomotive,
have been refuted by Stephenson's own method
of laying down the railroad and letting the cars
run. Innumerable solemnities, based on "the
divinely ordained nature of things," "on the
eternal justice" of woman's position now and
forever, world without end, have passed to the
limbo of many other solemnities which sink to
rise no more.

"The part played in this discussion by à *priori* arguments drawn from "the nature of things" and "eternal
justice," is alarming many sober-minded people as a speci-
men of the kind of thing to which female (?) legislators
would treat us." *

Let us contrast the position of women as it
existed in industry, in law, and in education
before 1848, and as it exists to-day.

* *Evening Post*, May 5, 1894.

II.

IN 1836 seven vocations only were open to women. They were allowed to be teachers, principally governesses; seamstresses, dressmakers, tailors, milliners, factory operatives, and household servants. In 1884 women were found employed in 354 subdivisions of industries. In 1892 Carroll Wright observes, "that there are but few avenues of remunerative employment which are not now open to women." The United States census of 1880 records for the entire country 2,666,000 women engaged in gainful occupations. This is about one fifth the number of men whose occupations are similarly classified. Owing to the imperfection of the census of 1890, it is impossible to form an exact estimate to-day. But, with the increased population, and in view of the fact that the increase of women in industrial occupations has been proportionately much greater than the increase in the population, the number of working women to-day must be considerably over three million.

" The entrance of women into the industrial field was assured, when, between 1760 and 1770, the factory system of labor displaced the hand-labor system." *

Three new ideas about women have become gradually, but irresistibly, established by the fact of their widespread participation in modern industry.

1st. That women are *not* universally supported by men, but, in very considerable numbers, support themselves all their lives ; in still larger numbers support themselves for many years of their lives, perhaps the largest part ; and also very frequently support also, in whole or in part, their children or other relatives. Impossible, therefore, to continue to look upon women as a universally dependent class. This, indeed, would never have been possible if the true significance of the work of woman had been recognized, when the textile and almost all other industries were carried on under the domestic roof. But women were then said not to contribute to production, but to be supported entirely by men,—merely because these indi-

* Carroll Wright, *Forum*, July, 1892.

vidually furnished the raw material for their industry; and because the work performed was part of the ordinary domestic labor of the household.

" There is no distinction in character between the work of the baker who provides bread for a family, and that of a cook who boils potatoes." *

2d. That the work of women, now so frequently and evidently non-domestic, could no longer be considered as something done exclusively in the personal service of father or husband ; it had become a recognized and important factor in the wealth of the State. From the moment of such recognition began to be undermined the theory which assumed that women only existed within their families, and had no direct relations with the State.

3d. That the individual protection of the man or men in the family was quite insufficient to shield the woman industrial in the various exigencies to which her employment gave rise. If laws were needed to defend the personal rights of any workman, laws were needed to defend women. But further, it could not fail to be observed that laws for the proper defence

* Marshall, *Principles of Economics*, pp. 117-119.

of men possessed of political rights were more easily obtained and more surely enforced than were analogous laws for women. Recent and vivid experience had demonstrated the steady improvement in the condition of the working-man which coincided with, and was somewhat proportioned to, his share in political privilege, —his power to make his wants known with a certain degree of authority. Impossible not to inquire why similar improvement should not follow the extension of political rights to working-women.

Though facts generate ideas, they do not affect social movements until the ideas about facts have changed. From 1760 and the Arkwright spinning-jenny, women, for good or ill, left their homes and passed into the factories. But until 1848 their earnings did not belong to themselves, at least not if they were married, which it was their normal condition to be. Hence the whole significance of the industrial situation remained veiled until, from another quarter, had been effected a revolution in the legal status of women.

It is not necessary to weight these few pages with even an allusion to such elaborate researches on the property rights and legal status

of women as won for Laboulaye the recompense
of the French Academy. It suffices to recall
the well-known dictum of Blackstone that,
according to the Common Law of England, " the
personality of the married woman [the *femme
couvert*] was entirely merged in that of her
husband."

" From the very beginning of history, woman appears
everywhere in a state of complete subordination.
Law . . . sanctions the subjection of woman. At
Rome—legislating for the universe—this tenet is formulated in the harshest terms. Christianity does little to
alter woman's position ; the Canon Law cannot forgive
her the seduction of Adam. ' Adam was beguiled by
Eve, not Eve by Adam. It is just that woman should
take as her ruler him whom she incited to sin, that he
may not fall a second time through female levity.'—
Decret. ii. The barbarian society which rises in the place
of the Greco-Roman world, founded as it was on force,
showed no greater willingness to recognize the personality of woman : her legal status is here one of perpetual
tutelage." *

Blackstone claimed that the disabilities which
the wife lies under were for the most part intended for her protection and benefit, " so great
a favorite is the female sex with the laws of
England." †

* Ostrogorski, *Rights of Women*, 1893.   † 1 *Comm.*, 4, p. 445.

Let us enumerate the proofs of such favoritism.

For the better protection of the woman, the
husband was forbidden to chastise his wife
with a stick bigger than his own thumb.

For her better support, all the property of
the wife, real and personal, was handed over
to the absolute control of the husband; all
rents, profits, and income from lands; all stocks,
bonds, plate, and furniture; the jewelry given
in girlhood by a mother; the very silver mug
which had been the gift of the sponsors in baptism.

For her greater security, or that of this same
property, a woman was prohibited from making
a will; in many instances from serving as a
witness; could give no power of attorney; make
no contract; neither sue nor be sued; nor engage in any business on her own account.

For her safer maintenance, it was provided
that any money she might earn must pass to her
husband, who had liberty to withdraw her
deposits at the savings-bank, even to find means
with which to purchase his liquor, or pay his
gambling debts.

For the better satisfaction of her maternal
instincts, the mother was obliged to leave her

child absolutely within the control of its father, if he chose to recognize it as his own; the mother was only certainly able to care for, educate, apprentice, or otherwise dispose of her child, if it had been born out of wedlock, and the father had deserted it. Only the child of a slave followed the condition of its mother,—and such child always did, so that the father was freed from all inconvenient responsibility for his illegitimate children, either white or black.

And to more securely hedge with respect female honor and chastity, a father was allowed to sue the seducer of his daughter for the money value of her services to him as a servant.

It was in the winter of 1848—the winter immediately following the Revolution and the Seneca Falls Convention—that the first steps were taken in that series of legislative enactments which has finally placed the women of the State of New York on a full legal equality with men. It is unnecessary to enumerate the successive steps, of which the last was no earlier than 1862. The important fact is that to-day a married woman has as complete control over her own property as the *femme sole*; is not liable for her husband's debts, unless by her own free will; can administer and devise her real estate and personal belongings; can make contracts even with her own husband; can enforce the absence of even ante-nuptial contracts with him; can sue and be sued; can engage in any business, and control her own earnings; is joint guardian of her child with its father; can forbid such education, religious or otherwise, as she disapproves; can forbid such apprenticeship as she deems unsuitable; and, in a word, has become an equal person in her own family, and joint ruler in her own house.

Comments upon these new laws often seem to imply that their value lay in securing better pecuniary provision for women. But such an interpretation would be always inadequate, sometimes contradictory to the facts, and always far below the real dignity of their significance.

" The taking up arms merely to enforce the repeal of a pecuniary law, seems as unwarrantable, and is as repugnant to the feelings, as the taking up arms to enforce obedience thereto." *

A woman, charged with the responsibility of her own estate, might indeed often fail to ad-

* *Common Sense*, p. 118.

minister it as well as trustees would have done;
or would make a will less reasonable than could
have been planned by her husband.   The property of heiresses could be secured by marriage
settlements so as to be safe from the recklessness or untouched by the business embarrass-
ments of husbands.   Indeed the security of the
property was liable to be in direct proportion
to its amount, as that amount was often in inverse proportion to the energy and necessity of
the woman possessing it.   The hardworking
washerwoman, driven to work to save herself
and children from starvation, had no security
for her little earnings;   the heiress could be
saved by the foresight of her father from the
consequences of either her husband's vices or
her own inexperience.   The change which increased the power of the poor woman, lessened
if anything the special privilege of the rich,
and tended to equalize their respective conditions by throwing each woman on her own
resources and own responsibility.   This was
the great thing accomplished: the personality
of the woman was distinctly disengaged, recognized, and established before the law on equal
terms with that of the man.   For her who had
been hitherto thoroughly protected, whose cir-

cumstances were entirely favorable, whose
enervating education had unfitted her for acts
of independent judgment and for positions of
grave responsibility,—in a word, for the typical
woman of the pathetic novel, the new law may
be said to have imposed a burden considerably
greater than that now dreaded by some of the
opponents of equal suffrage. But for all others
it was a boon, a conquest, whose ideal effects
are only at this moment beginning to be thoroughly felt and apprehended. The difference
between equal rights to children, property,
and independence, guaranteed by law, and privileges accorded by courtesy, or even affection,
is precisely the difference between the position
of the freeman and the serf, and affects at last
not only the tangible matters which may or
may not come into dispute, but the intangible
moral atmosphere which surrounds each individual during every hour of his life.

"In the present state of America . . . we are
without . . . any other mode of power than what is
founded on and granted by courtesy." *

I have used the word serf instead of slave, so
as to avoid the appearance of exaggeration, in

* *Common Sense.* p. 126.

speaking of the legal disabilities of women, which were removed between 1848 and 1862.

Yet this peculiar status of married women really combined the disabilities of both serf and slave. Like the former, she did not own land, or any other property; she was attached to it. And, like the slave, she might slave from dawn to dusk, yet have no right to a farthing of the products of her own labor; no equivalent, indeed, except a claim for a maintenance whose details should be determined by a master. The fact was concealed by the social habits and manners which had become modified, as usual, in advance of the law. But the fact remained, and was disclosed as soon as looked for, that in the eye of the law the married white woman in the North was as devoid of personality as the African slave in the South.

Thus a second line of thought and inquiry led straight to the same startling conclusion as had already been reached by the abolitionists along a somewhat different route. A class of people who were not allowed to be persons, were found to have existed on the north of Mason and Dixon's line, as well as on the south. The first measure to establish the personality of the woman, coincided with the opening of the struggle for the negro, and was carried largely

by the efforts of the same people as were working for him. The final step was taken by the
laws of 1862, 1878, 1884, and 1887, nearly all
enacted long after the passage of the Fourteenth
and Fifteenth Amendments. Yet, in a large
historic grouping it may be averred that the
same epoch conferred the gift of personality
upon the married woman of New York and
upon the slave of South Carolina.

This is the real meaning of the great reform
legislation for women of the State of New York.

Thus again, not through rhetorical exaggeration, but through the line of sequence of historic
fact, are we led to find in the political emancipation of the negroes a substantial precedent for the
political emancipation of women,—because justified by the same ideal necessity. From many
points of view, it certainly seemed most absurd
to invite to a share in the Popular Sovereignty a
million negroes only just emancipated from two
hundred years of bondage,—and who, moreover,
had not themselves dreamed of demanding
more than their personal liberty, their "forty
acres and a mule."

" The unpatriotic remonstrants are willing to sacrifice
justice and every principle of self-government to a
masterly inactivity and blissful self-content." *

* *Rochester Herald*, May 4, 1894.

Nevertheless the heroic measure embodied in the Fifteenth Amendment was absolutely necessary in order to convince the former masters that their former chattels had really become men. Possession of personal liberty, personal equality before the law, would not have sufficed to drive home the conviction.

When, turning from the negro, we begin to speak of the women, we rise out of an atmosphere absolutely black, into one which is only gray—sometimes a very light gray—or even ashes of roses. Nevertheless, for the women it is—as for the slave it would have been true, that, in the absence of political right, legal emancipation has not sufficed to bring them to a condition of full personality in the social estimate. The very horror so often expressed, or thinly veiled under more polite expression, at the possibility that the will of women, as exerted through their votes, might occasionally prevail, is sufficient proof of this. Even American women are *not* felt to be persons in the same sense as the male immigrants among the Hungarians, Poles, Russian Jews,—not to speak of Italians, Germans, and the masters of all of us—the Irish !

" Let us sum up South Dakota. The total vote was 70,000, of whom 30,000 were foreigners—Scandinavians,

Swedes, Norwegians, Russians,—all classes. Of the American-born men, 24,000 voted yes (for the woman-suffrage amendment), and 16,000 voted no. But the 30,000 foreigners' vote was added to the 16,000, and that made a tremendous majority against us." *

It remains to correct two errors of interpretation.

It is often asserted that the legislation of 1848 rectified certain grave "wrongs" which women had hitherto suffered. Not a few people argue, that, since the "legal wrongs" of women have been so effectually remedied without the suffrage, suffrage for women is superfluous, and should, therefore, be neither asked nor accorded.

But these laws embodied no "wrongs" to women, except in so far as it could be considered a wrong to deny her personality. The laws which were abolished, had been enacted under the more or less honest belief that a woman could never attain the measure of a full-grown adult personality; was permanently in the condition of a child, and therefore really required a guardian, protector, and champion. That the guardian might profit by his ward, and the champion be only too well protected by the fortune of his protégée, was a trifling incident easily overlooked.

* Susan B. Anthony. Speech at Leavenworth, May 4, 1894.

The legal independence of unmarried women was regarded as a real misfortune, and to be made as nominal as possible by various contrivances of trustees and other guardianship. In any case, it was agreed to consider spinsterhood as an abnormality of small proportions and small consequence, something like an extra finger or two on the body, presumably of temporary duration, and never of any social significance.

The theory of championship only slowly faded away with the recession of the ages of physical violence, where the need of a champion was plausible; or rather it began to fade a good many centuries after this plausibility had vanished. It then gradually dawned on the social consciousness—or, more specifically, it was driven into the understandings of the New York Legislature by the strenuous efforts of Mrs. Stanton, Miss Anthony, and their fellow suffragists—that women were, after all, persons, and that the obliteration or merging of their personality inflicted on them a wrong, greater than any benefit which could accrue from entrusting the management of their property to more experienced hands than their own.

By another error of interpretation, certain laws which remain on the Statute Book, or which have been recently added, have been considered so peculiarly favorable to women, that they are thought to prove a legislative tendency to grant special immunities to women so long as these consent to remain unenfranchised. The fear has been expressed, that these "immunities" and "privileges" would be forfeited were the franchise conferred. And this fear has actually been advanced as an argument—as the basis of protest against the equal suffrage.

The laws cited are : the dower right of wives in the real estate of their husbands; the requirement of the wife's signature to deeds of purchase or sale of real estate executed by the husband, while the wife is at liberty, unchecked, to dispose of her own property.

Those "dower rights" are founded on the claim of a wife to maintenance for herself and the children she has borne, to the extent of securing a home for them. Through the veto power on a sale vested in her, the wife may, when necessary, be enabled to guard and save the inheritance of her children. A woman's legal claim for maintenance as a wife lies within very narrow limits, and it is just that it should do so. Only as a mother can such claim be preferred with either justice or dignity; and here it should often be far larger than is, in the great majority of cases in practical life, really admitted. As there is no reason why a wife should ever " maintain " her husband, so there is no reason now why she should not dispose of her property as she please.

The laws which, after long struggle and occasional repeal, finally accorded to the mother equal rights with the father over the child, have a special significance which we believe has been hitherto overlooked.

" In 1860 an equal guardianship over the children was accorded to husband and wife. But in 1862 this law was repealed, and a man's widow was no longer allowed to be *ipso facto* guardian of her own children. In 1871, however, the Surrogate was allowed to appoint guardians, as hitherto only the Supreme Court had been able to do ; and under this law, the custody of minor children is commonly awarded to the mother." *

This group of laws, which forbids a father to educate or apprentice his child without the consent of the mother, and which gives to the mother equal guardianship over the child during the life, and practically complete guardianship after the death of the father, is a reflex, most unconsciously to the lawgivers, of a great physio-

* Laws of the State of New York Affecting Women. Suffrage Leaflets, Committee 11th Assembly District.

logical discovery. Until 1827 it had been always supposed that the mother had no essential share in the formation of the child's organism. It was supposed that the mother's body only furnished the soil upon which the embryo, exclusively generated by the father, might develop; that her blood yielded nutriment, but that no essential elements of the new being were derived from her. In 1827 Von Baer discovered the ovule, the reproductive cell of the maternal organism, and demonstrated that its protoplasm contributed at least one half to the tissues of the embryo. From this moment was established the theory of equal maternal inheritance for the child, and, as a necessary correlative, an equality of control over the child for the mother.

Thus does the Idea, born in obscurity and solitude, descend slowly from its far-off lonely heights, and finally take possession of the world!

There is a third group of laws, where the alleged "favoritism" is an acknowledgment either of the inferior physical strength of women, or of her unequal position as compared with fellow-workers who are allowed to defend their interests through the ballot. Under the first heading comes, very obviously, the "immunity" of a woman from an order of sheriff or officer

3

of the peace to assist in quelling a disturbance
or in making an arrest; from the obligation to
take up arms in defence of law and authority;
also the limits placed on the liability of arrest
of women for civil or criminal suits. The factory laws, framed for the protection of women,
and which so often fail to do so, have a triple
significance. They propose to defend the class
of industrials who have no political representation; to protect the sex incapable of physical
self-assertion; and finally, and more especially,
to save from ruinous exhaustion the mothers
who must bear and rear for the State thousands
of its citizens. The ninety years' struggle,
(beginning in England in 1802), which has
been needed to enact and partially enforce these
factory laws; the stubborn resistance which, in
New York State, has been offered to all proposals to submit to the operation of such laws
the masses of female industrials outside of factories, as in retail stores, and who also need
such protection,—all indicate the extreme difficulty of securing protection for any class of
people who have not either directly, by the
ballot, or indirectly through its strengthening
educational influence, been put in a position to
protect themselves.

There is finally one law about which a great deal has been said in recent current debates, which cannot be referred to any of the three foregoing classes. This is the law obliging men who cannot offer especial excuse to serve once a year on juries. The opponents to equal suffrage have constantly cited woman's present exemption from this citizen duty as a proof of her favored position ; while the friends of the suffrage have usually been content to reply that woman might be made exempt by special legislation, and that, as a matter of fact, after some trial, women had been so exempted in Wyoming.

I think this reply is both feeble and fallacious. Certainly if women claim to exercise the functions of sovereignty, they must be prepared to assume a fair share of the public duties of citizenship. Precisely because they must be exempted from military and constable duty, where they would be of no use, should women be expected to hold themselves in readiness to fulfil such functions as those of jurors, which demand only the minimum amount of physical strength, and which appeal chiefly to reason, judgment, and fidelity. As the court-rooms are habitually thronged all day with women who do nothing but idle in them, and it has not yet

been proposed to send such women to the sanc-
tity of their own homes, by either decree of
law or force of police, some other reason than
physical infirmity must be found to exclude
women from the jurors' box. The plausible
reasons are two : First, that women are not
sufficiently trained in the art of reasoning to
follow an argument, and their minds have not
such calibre that their judgment can be relied
upon. Secondly, that it would be indecorous
and unseemly to shut up together women and
men jurors, strangers to each other, coming from
different ranks of society, yet compelled for
hours, days, or even weeks to remain closely
associated together; talking, arguing together,
trying to persuade each other, or submitting to
be persuaded. The vision of jury duty which
very naturally rises in the mind at the suggestion that women might be called to engage in
it, concentrates in itself all the objection, in all
its intensity, that can be raised or felt to the
participation of women in responsible public
affairs. In this one illustration is concentrated
all objection based on the immemorable distrust of female intelligence, and all due to the
immemorable conventions of female decorum.
Yet, precisely because these objections are very

old, may it be suspected that they are beginning
to be somewhat worn out.

For the jury, as for the ballot, the level of the
average qualification renders absurd the assumption that there are not already thousands of
women, educated and clear-headed, at least as
fitted for a jury as the men who are now im-
panelled. Jury duty, properly prepared for
and honestly performed, would itself constitute
a most valuable training for women, intellectually, morally, and socially. For them, as for the
Athenian people in the days of Pericles, who
first made the observation, the performance of
jury duty is one of the best methods of becoming practically acquainted with the laws of the
State. It has been shown that women physicians were useful, because women patients
abounded. Similarly, if women are now called
into court as clients, witnesses, accused, and
spectators, it is impossible to maintain that law-
suits and contested rights do not concern women.
The Anglo-Saxon jury—differing in that from
the Athenian—was simply a body of witnesses
to fact ; and women—whose testimony in certain ages and countries has not been admitted
as legal evidence—are now permitted to so tes-
tify. From this permission to that of judging

testimony; from the witness-stand to the jury-
box, is, literally, but a step.

The objection in regard to decorum is at once
more subtle and more powerful, for a given
standard of decorum constitutes an all-pervading
mental atmosphere, whose influence is as difficult to escape as to controvert. It can only be
outgrown as ideals of decorum become modified, or as different methods become devised in
order to realize the same ideals. In this specific
problem of jurors, no matter what degree of
separation between the male and female members might be provided, some degree of association is necessitated by the very nature of the
jurors' duty, which involves mutual and sometimes protracted and heated discussion. Doubt-
less the association together of men and women
in such discussion has only become possible at
the present day, when manners have become
sufficiently softened, and the habit of decorous
commingling of the sexes has been sufficiently
well established. But, these conditions being
premised, as who can doubt, the situation *has*
become possible; and it is easy to foresee many
special advantages that would soon accrue to
such mixed juries, where a group of honest
men and women were united for the high pur

pose of securing justice. The admission to the jury of immoral persons of either sex could only be due to remissness in challenging ; as it is already customary to exclude persons whose character can be called in question.

The numerous causes for exemption now admitted for men would be certainly paralleled for women, but they would not always be identical. Men are now more often excused for business ; women would more often be excused on the plea of ill-health. Of course, the special plea of family cares with young children would rule out thousands of women during a certain number of years of their lives. These same women, however, would often make valuable jurors, when their nurseries had emptied and their children were grown up.

Even more conspicuous and wide-reaching than the changes in the industrial and legal status of women, are the changes which since 1848 have been effected in the educational opportunities accessible to the female sex.

Within twenty years from the landing of the Pilgrims at Plymouth, the foundation of the free-school system was laid, but *not* for girls. For nearly a century and a half the girls had no education beyond what they might pick up at

home or by the aid of a minister. In 1771 girls
were admitted, for the first time, to the common
schools at Hartford, Conn., and there taught
reading, writing, spelling, and the catechism.
The boys studied the first four rules of arithmetic, but to these mysteries the girls had no
access. When at last they were allowed to
study arithmetic, they were limited to addition, and forbidden to consider the other three
rules. In 1790, at Newburyport, a proposition
to provide schools for girls was put aside without action by the town. In 1804, female children over nine years of age were allowed to attend school between six and eight in the morning, and on Thursday afternoon. Not till 1836
did the school committee deem that one female
grammar school should be kept open throughout the year. One taxpayer objected to this
decision, and applied for an injunction, bringing
out Judge Shaw's celebrated opinion on that
point.*

In the law of 1789, the expression "master
and mistress" recognizes women as teachers for
the first time.† Hitherto women so employed

---

* The above and many following details are taken from the most
interesting monograph by Mary Eastman, in *Woman's Work in
America*. Henry Holt, 1891.

† Significant date—that of the foundation of the American Constitution !

could not legally collect their wages; the receipt of their dues depended upon the honor of their employers.

"They were without other mode of power than what is founded on and granted by courtesy."

Although excluded from common schools, or receiving only the scantiest instructions in them, girls began in the middle of the eighteenth century to be provided with private academies and seminaries; and finally, in 1821, Mrs. Willard succeeded in establishing the famous Troy Seminary, the first institution for girls that approached the level of a high-school.

In 1825 an attempt was made to establish a city high-school for girls in Boston, but the school was closed at the end of a year, *because* such a large number of girls entered, and stayed so long that "no funds of any city could endure the expense." For *girls*, that is—for the boys' English high-school had been supported for four years, and the Latin school during nearly two centuries, out of the public funds, and without protest from the citizens.

In 1852 a Normal school for girls was established in Massachusetts; in 1878 the girls' Latin school; and in 1888 one hundred and ninety-eight cities and towns in the State supported

high-schools, most of which were co-educational.
The Mount Holyoke Seminary, the immediate
successor to that at Troy, was opened in 1837
by Miss Lyon, in spite of the opposition of the
clergy.

"You see that the measure has utterly failed. Let this
page of Divine Providence be attentively considered in
relation to this matter ! " *

In the West, Oberlin College began its work
in 1833 ; Antioch in 1853 ; and throughout the
Western States, the universities, founded upon
the land funds created by the ordinance of
1787, began to admit women between 1861 and
1871 ; all organized since the latter date have
started out as co-educational institutions. † In
New York State, after the foundation of Troy
Seminary, there was no new institution until
1865, when the Vassar Collége was opened at
Poughkeepsie. By 1890, Vassar had conferred
a degree upon eight hundred or nine hundred
graduates. Smith College was founded at
Northampton, Mass., in 1868; Wellesley in
1875; Bryn Mawr, in Pennsylvania, in 1885.
But in 1872 women were admitted on the same

* Cited by Miss Eastman, *loc. cit.*
† *Woman's Work in America: Education in Western States.*
May Wright Sewall.

terms with men to the Cornell State University; in 1879 touched upon Harvard, through the intermediary of the "annex"; in 1889 entered the post-graduate courses of the University of Pennsylvania; and in the same year, Barnard College was formally opened, in close associàtion with Columbia. The Massachusetts Institute of Technology has received women since 1883; and women were admitted to the post-graduate courses at Yale about ten years later.

In the Southern States, opportunities for first-class university education hardly exist for women. Yet there are in the South one hundred and fifty institutions holding the nominal grade of college, which are authorized by Legislature to confer degrees upon women. At the Johns Hopkins University of Baltimore no woman has yet been admitted to the faculty of arts; but, in reverse of the usual order, the medical school has been thrown open to women, in order to be able to utilize the munificent donation* made by a woman on this condition, and which alone enabled the school to be founded.

Nor has the educational movement for women been confined to the United States. All over Europe except in Germany, and, with

* $500,000 given by Miss Garrett.

capricious exceptions, in Russia, the universities have been open to women. In England special colleges for women have been established at Cambridge and Oxford, affording the same in-struction and conferring equivalent degrees to those given at the university itself. Since 1872 four thousand women have received degrees from the University of London, and everywhere that the opportunity has been afforded to com-pete, the women have carried off, in proportion to their numbers, a larger share of honors than men.

The professional education of women is, for the purpose of this pamphlet, the most impor-tant of the whole, because marking most dis-tinctly a revolution in ideas. Although untrue in fact, it was conceivable, that even university education might be regarded as destined exclu-sively to embellish women as ladies; as Latin had been taught in England only for the pur-pose of "finishing" a gentleman.

Horace Mann had said in 1836 that the se-cluded life to which women were naturally destined, especially required the resources of a liberal education for its embellishment and dis-traction. The enunciation of this truth, which to-day seems so innocent and obvious, was, however, a radical innovation upon the views hitherto held.

" Il n'est pas bien honnête, et pour beaucoup de causes,
Qu'une femme étudie et sache tant de choses.

.   .   .   .

Nos pères, sur ce point, étaient gens bien sensés,
Qui disaient qu'une femme en sait toujours assez
Quand la capacité de son esprit se hausse,
À connaître un pourpoint d'avec un haut-de-chausse." *

But when the education received by girls, began to be turned to practical account, the innovation became more decided.

Of the four professions into which, so far, women have entered for the purpose of earning their livings—teaching, medicine, law, and journalism,—the first was the earliest invaded and has always, from the beginning, been the most thronged. To the initiative of two women teachers, Emma Willard and Mary Lyon, had been indeed due the earliest steps in the movement to secure any real education for women. The positions of governess, half nurse and half companion, had been long established in Europe, among wealthy families, and imported to a limited extent into this country. But the systematic training of women for teaching as a

* *Les Femmes Savantes*, Act II., Scene VII.

profession, the establishment for them of Normal Schools, their installation by the thousand in charge of the public schools of the entire country,—this marked a transition as great as would be effected by transforming a private lacquey into a public official.

The census of 1880 records over 100,000 women as teachers, in the public schools of the country.

The census of 1890 is too imperfect for classified occupations.

The public-school teachers are public officials in a double sense. They train the children, boys as well as girls, who are to become citizens of the State. They are themselves marshalled, superintended, and governed by officers who have been elected by the voters of the State at regular occasions appointed for the exercise of functions of sovereignty. The more developed becomes the science and art of pedagogy, the more does the profession of teaching become a matter of expertise, and the successful teacher a person of trained and proved capacity. Such capacity may often be intellectually superior to that of the administrative capacity required in the elected officials; and is avowedly superior to that of the average voter who elects them.

Yet the female teachers have no vote. For this very reason they are habitually excluded from the upper positions with the larger salaries, and are officially excluded from aspiring to the administrative positions only obtainable by election.

Here is a pyramid resting on its weakest part, standing absolutely topsy-turvy. Not only this army of teachers, but all other women, presumably attached by special affiliations to the schools, and unquestionably profoundly interested in the children taught, are largely forbidden to exercise either supervision or control over either the instruction, or the fortunes of those who instruct. In twelve States of the Union, the right of school suffrage has, after long controversy, been conceded to women. In the State of New York, however, though permitted in some localities to vote for School Trustees, women have, by the decision of the Supreme Court, handed down in January, 1894, been pronounced unable to vote for School Commissioner, until they shall have been relieved of their disability through a constitutional amendment.

This decision has precipitated the movement to obtain from the constitutional convention now in session, an amendment which shall rectify

the disturbed balance of things, and enable women to vote, whenever they have a wish to express, and a legitimate interest to defend; an
amendment which may put an end to the confusion of ideas which engenders injustice, and
to a confusion of responsibilities which invites
neglect.

Useless to say with tentative conservatism,
"To women the child and the training of the
child and the schooling of the child, and
therefore, School Suffrage." In the immense
cities of Brooklyn and New York, even the
limited right to vote for school trustees does
not exist,—for the ward trustees are appointed
through local elections, and the Board of Education is nominated by the Mayor. The appropriations for the schools, the expenditures
of these appropriations, to which taxation on
property owned by women contributes in large
proportion, are decided by Boards of Estimate
and other officials, with whose selection not a
mother in these vast populations has a word to
say.

Yet it is more logical for the State of New
York to declare women unable to elect School
commissioners until they shall have been
clothed with full rights of sovereignty, than .

it is for Massachusetts to pronounce women fit to vote for school officials but unfit to vote for any one else.

The decision of the Supreme Court, like the ship-money levied in the inland county of Hampshire, has served, we repeat, to precipitate a discussion so radical, that it will not cease until the irresistible claims of logic are satisfied. Nor will such satisfaction be, as has been asserted, "too French" in its completeness. It will fully continue the English march of thought we cherish as our own, which

"Broadens slowly down from precedent to precedent."

The profession of medicine was thrown open to women when, in 1849, the year following the Revolution, and the Woman's Rights Convention, and the passage of the Married Woman's Property Bill, New York State for the first time, at Geneva, conferred a medical diploma on a woman, Elizabeth Blackwell. She was, or rather became, the sister-in-law of Lucy Stone ; and the work of these two women, the one in medicine, the other for equal suffrage, constituted the two necessary halves of one idea. If all women were to claim such substantial equality with men, as was implied

in equality of political right, it was essential
that some women should prove themselves
to be capable of work which involved the highest intellectual and social responsibilities.

It was an arduous task for the women of
fifty years ago, starting from the low level of
the education which had up to that time been
alone accessible to them, to show any capacity,
or even the dimmest insight into the great intellectual province of medicine.   But the difficulty
of the task was immensely magnified by the
intense hostility aroused in the profession
against the admission of women to its ranks.
The history of this acrimonious controversy is
that of a pitched battle, whose echoes have
· hardly yet died away.

> "So all day long the noise of battle rolled,
>   Among the mountains by the winter sea."

"Those accustomed to value ideas according to their
intrinsic power, as shown by their originality and fruitful
result, should admit that there was real grandeur in this
thought ; the thought that the entire sex might be lifted
upon a higher intellectual plane by means of a practical
work, for which at the moment not half a dozen people
in America discerned the oppportunity." *

Nothing is more intrinsically remote from
political rights and interests than the sphere of

* "Women in Medicine," *Women's Work in America*, p. 150.

medicine; yet, because political equality implies average equality between the sexes, and admission to an intellectual profession concedes the possibility of even intellectual superiority among women, the arguments by which this admission was opposed and retarded are identical with many of those to-day advanced against woman suffrage. It is true that detailed argument on a legitimate basis soon broke down, and resolutions were substituted which declared the views of the Supreme Being in regard to female physicians. But such substitution is paralleled in our time also. In 1871, at the American Medical Association, an Illinois doctor asked very solemnly whether "the time had come, by deliberate action to open the door and welcome the female portion of the community, not only into our profession, but into all professions. Do we desire this time ever to come? Is there any difference in the sexes? Were they designed for any different spheres? Are we to heed the law plainly imprinted on the human race,—or are we, as a body, to yield to the popular breeze of the times, and say it must come, and therefore we will do it?" Apparently that is exactly what this august body finally did do.

Therefore the friends of equal rights for women must not feel too discouraged when, nearly twenty-five years later, in a somewhat different sphere, another note of warning was raised with equal piety and solemnity. (?)

"Another matter which lies deeply imbedded in the entire Scriptural record, is the essential disparity of the two sexes. . . . The intention of Scripture is clear from the method in which it handles representatives of the womanly sex. . . . Any civilization that transforms or tends to transform a woman into the female duplicate of a man, is a false civilization. [Yet] you would have no logical warrant for deciding that because the Virgin Mary does not seem to have turned over the miraculous babe into the clumsy keeping of Joseph in order to get opportunity to skip to the polls, therefore mothers of our own era and city are morally restrained from oscillating between the crib and the ballot-box." *

At the present day women are members of medical societies of the highest rank all over the United States; support three large schools of their own and several lesser ones; are admitted to the medical schools of all the Western State Universities; and in the East to the school of the Johns Hopkins University. Women·have graduated from these schools to

* Rev. Dr. Parkhurst, sermon preached May 13, 1894. *Tribune*, May 14th.

the number of several thousand, practise all
over the United States, study with varying
degrees of freedom in hundreds of hospitals, and
conduct seven of their own. The legal status
of women in medicine is absolutely the same as
that of men; they are eligible for all State
appointments, fill official positions on health
boards, in prisons, and reformatories, and—by
special legislation recently enacted in several
States, including New York—are specifically
ordered for appointment in female insane
asylums. Their expert testimony, already accepted by life-insurance companies, is recognized in law courts. And by a special amendment to a New York law of 1893, judges are
empowered to order the physical examinations
of female contestants by women physicians,
who are then said to be clothed with "quasi-
judicial functions."

The admission of women to the profession of
law does not indicate the attainment of any
higher intellectual standard than is implied
by their introduction into medicine, but it has
a special significance of its own. Medicine,
though recognized, employed, and to some
extent controlled by the State, remains chiefly
a matter of private, and at most of social, con-

cern. But it is different with law. In 1883 the Supreme Court of Italy decided that " the function of advocate constituted something more than a profession; it was a kind of public and necessary office; and, to admit women to the Bar, was required a formal test declaring women capable of holding all offices and all appointments, both public and civil." *

In 1888 the court at Brussels decided in the same way, "that a woman could only be an advocate, if she is capable of filling the office of judge."

" Oh, wise young judge, how I do honour thee ! "

"In conclusion the Procureur-General declared that in the present state of legislation and opinion, women could neither hold the title nor exercise the profession of advocate, and that on the day when they were admitted to the Bar, there would be an end to the independence and dignity of the Bar." †

Notwithstanding these recent and learned opinions pronounced by the Supreme Courts of two great European countries, the various States of the American Union, after a certain amount

* *Rights of Women*, Ostrogorski, 1893, p. 144.
† Ostrogorski, *loc. cit.*, p. 146.

of controversy over specific demands for admission, have generally pronounced women eligible for the profession. "When the law courts resisted, legislature intervened in favor of women. Special laws authorizing them to practise as advocates were adopted in the following States: California (Constitution), Illinois (1881), Iowa (1882), Massachusetts, Minnesota (1881), New York (1886), Ohio (1879), Wisconsin (1878), Massachusetts (1882). Last in importance, though not in order of time, a federal law, adopted February 13, 1879, has given women access to the Bar of the Supreme Court of the United States." [*]

In other spheres woman's practical work has much antedated its own official recognition. In law the State has gone faster in admitting women to the Bar than they in pressing forward to come in. The close association of legal occupations with political rights, the intimate connections between the law and its administration, and the political structure of society, should both explain and justify this rational delay. Possibly women may always remain *rari nantes* in this profession, to which no such special calls for them exist as in the profession of medi-

[*] Ostrogorski, *loc. cit.*, p. 159.

cine. But there is an intrinsic absurdity in the
active practice of law by women who do not
possess the ballot: there is too glaring a contradiction in the proposal to admit women advocates to plead in the same court-room whence
women jurors are excluded. Italy and Bel- ·
gium have been logical in pointing out this
inconsistency. If the United States has overlooked it, we may accept the fact as an indica-
tion of another fact of which the judges of even
the Supreme Court seem to be unconscious, that
the day of women's political enfranchisement is
near at hand,—is standing at the door.

Upon the profession of journalism it is unnecessary to dwell at length. The extensive
admission of women into this profession is significant, not to the extent to which journalism
touches upon literature, for the point of contact
is very slight, but to the modern position of
the daily press as a powerful factor in moulding public opinion.

In a society where government is founded
upon and conducted by public opinion, in the
profession which stands almost as closely allied
to this, as do laws to political institutions,
women are admitted—women throng.

Their opportunities for rising are limited

chiefly by their ability. Their ability is ener-
vated, not only by other causes, but by the
remoteness from actual affairs proper to an
unenfranchised, a politically alien class. Still, in
journalism, there the women are, there they seem
destined to stay ; there, in small ways, so multiple as almost to become an equivalent for
ways larger and fewer, they exercise a public
influence. How is it possible much longer for
the new right to remain unattended by its co-
relative responsibility ?

" The authority of Great Britain over this country is a
form of government which, sooner or later, must have an
end." *

Government has established special and entirely new relations with women along all the
lines of new work above described. It has protected women operatives by factory laws ; it has
accorded women in business, rights in contracts
and personal rights hitherto withheld. It has
enforced the admittance of women to all public
institutions for education, from the primary
school to the State University ; it has entrusted
public education and the training of citizens
chiefly to women ; it has legalized the position

* *Common Sense*, p. 84.

of women in the learned professions ; and it has
thrown open to women a large number of
official positions and salaried employments.
Seven thousand women are to-day employed
in the various administration offices at Washington, where, however, it is deemed necessary
even by their friends, to keep for them a certain
inferiority of position or salary, lest their places
should be claimed by voters. This close relation of women to appointed official position
brings them within a stone's throw of elected
official position,—certainly within a step of
the position of sharing in the election.

"The civil-service law practically went into effect in
1883. The report for 1884 stated that while the 'law'
made no distinction on account of sex, the 'appointing
power' had thus far used its discretion in the selection
from the list of eligibles of less than one-sixth as many
women as men, *although a larger proportion of female than
male competitors passed.* . . . In the year 1891-'92
the number of women appointed in certain departments
showed a proportion of women to men of a little more
than 1 in 3, a very decided gain for women. This remarkable increase in the number of women appointed
and promoted is mainly explained by the extension of the
merit system at the civil-service examinations throughout
the country : a higher general average of marks is scored
by women than by men, except in the more difficult
technical examinations. . . . In the tabulated record

from January, 1886, to June, 1892, the women were only 12 % of the number examined, yet 77 % of them passed, as against some 60 % of the men. The civil-service commission closes its report with the remark that these records show when women in the public service have a fair and even chance with men, they win their full share of the more lucrative and responsible positions." *

* *Evening Post*, 1894.

III.

THIS fourfold strand of circumstance, this fourfold revolution in the industrial, legal, educational, and governmental position of women, has entirely changed the existing situation from that when the argument for equal suffrage was first outlined. Then the argument was sketched on thin and rarefied air; now it is embedded in solidities of accomplished fact. Then it only appealed to those whose ears were attuned to the finer vibrations beyond the diapasons of ordinary thought; to-day it is enforced by the practical exigencies of every-day life. Then it only based itself on the abstract principles dear to the elect souls,— among the great and good of all ages*; to-day the Thought has descended from the empyrean, it has taken flesh, it has become incarnate among the prosaic possibilities of men. It was

---

* "And for company the great and good of all ages."—Emerson in the *American Scholar*.

a Thought ; it has become an imminent Fact.
It was a Right; it has become an Expediency.
It was born a heavenly body of abstract Truth ;
it has become an earthly body of social and
political Institution.

" The propriety of woman suffrage in some
form or other is no longer a question of purely
speculative interest. In England for nearly
twenty years municipal suffrage has been enjoyed by unmarried women who are property
holders. In Utah Territory, since its organization, women have, until recently, been entitled
to vote, and are now deprived of that power by
act of Congress for reasons only of local and
not of general application. In Wyoming Territory and Washington Territory woman suffrage has been an assured success, and only the
constitutionality and not the wisdom of the law
granting it has ever been questioned. In Kansas, with its population of nearly one million,
women have been granted municipal suffrage
on the same terms with men, and at the elections held last spring voted in large numbers.
In New York and Maine similar bills have
within the year passed the Senate, though they
have been subsequently rejected by the House.
In our own (Massachusetts) Legislature a bill

granting municipal suffrage to women has for several years been favorably reported from the committee, and has secured a large vote in favor of its passage. Woman suffrage, whatever it may have been in the past, is to-day a question of practical politics." *

It is a practical question in America, in England, and the English colonies, among which New Zealand has just taken the lead in granting full suffrage to women. It is not yet a practical question in France, Germany, Austria, or the Latin States on the Mediterranean. Marked general inferiority of education; numerous restrictions on personal liberty, embodying a rooted disbelief in the possibility that commingling of the sexes can ever remain decorous if once allowed to be free; the persistence of civil disabilities which in America, and especially in the State of New York, would appear like a double anachronism pertaining to feudalism or to the Canon Law;—all these circumstances combine to restrain the movement for political rights for women, as yet, within "the sphere of the ridiculous." † Napoleon has said: "There is one thing that is not French,

* *Woman and the Commonwealth ; or, A Question of Expediency.* George Pellew, Boston, 1888.

† Ostrogorski, *loc. cit.*

and that is that a woman can do what she pleases."

" Some timid attempts made in the French Parliament to do away with the restrictions on the civil capacity of women have come to nothing. A Bill to grant women the right to be witnesses to deeds and to be guardians, though long since adopted by one of the two Chambers, is still in abeyance. Other Bills,—as for example, proposals for doing away with the prohibition of the quest as to the fathership have no chance of being adopted * ; there are too many lawyers in the French Chambers who have been brought up in a superstitious and blunt respect for the Code Napoleon." †

Notwithstanding the depression of women's civil rights, and their absolute exclusion from even the dream of political sphere, the women of France engage more freely than anywhere else in business and industry. In France, also, if anywhere, is the personal influence of women over men, both licit and illicit, most extensive, most openly acknowledged, most often disas-trous. The restrictions imposed upon women by law, often read like a half-despairing attempt on the part of men, to collectively revenge this

---

* This famous law on the *Recherché de la Paternité* is, neverthe-less, the object of constant witticisms among the French themselves. " In this way," it has been said, " do Frenchmen bind themselves together to support each other's children."

† Ostrogorski, *loc cit.*

influence, which they find themselves unable,
individually, to resist. The punishment is inflicted at the point where disaster arises,—on
whatever involves, directly or remotely, special
relations of sex. In regard to property, the
unmarried woman inherits the equal rights of
the Roman law rather than, as in England, the
feudal disabilities of daughters and sisters.
But in marital rights, in the claims of unmarried
maternity, in everything pertaining to the personal dignity of the individual woman which
might tend to raise her to an equality with
man—here the law is pitiless and society cruel.

Strange, therefore, in view of these obvious
and well-known facts to hear an American
writer denounce the extension of political rights
to women, lest, in the ardor of political strife,
women should appeal to "the potency of feminine charms, aided by feminine arts." The
woman "inside politics" will not fail to make
use of an influence so subtile and strong, and
of which the management is peculiarly suited
to her talents. When "woman is fairly 'inside politics,' the sensation press will reap a
harvest of scandals more lucrative to itself than
profitable to public morals." *

* Francis Parkman, *Some of the Reasons against Woman Suffrage.*

If experience can prove anything, it proves that the danger of illicit sex influences is, and always has been, in inverse proportion to the degree to which women approximated to equality with men, in social dignity and in opportunity for public responsibility. The women of the nation, or of the class, whose range of thought and sphere of action is most nearly reduced within the limits of sex relation, are liable to become dangerous precisely in proportion to the degree of such restriction. To the Anglo-Saxon race seems to have been especially committed the mission of securing and developing political freedom among men. Inadequate, defective in many other spheres, in this it has been invariably foremost and easily supreme. Their women cannot fail to share, at least to some extent, in the inherited instinct of the race and in its especial and accumulated capacity. It is among the nations of this race and its Scandinavian kindred that women have been and are most free, and have enjoyed the most many-sided development. The edict of the second Brumaire, which dissolved the female clubs of Paris, and sent hysteric termagants packing to their homes, contains no more forecast for the political possibilities of Anglo-Saxon women,

5

than do the masculine hysterics of the entire French Revolution forebode anything of the political future of England or America. "Bon chien chasse de race."

IV

RISE OF CAPACITY OF WOMEN, FALL OF POLITICAL
DIGNITY OF MEN.

A S in a mass of water into which a warm
current is let in below and slowly rises,
a cold and surface current as steadily descends;
so, during the fateful fifty years whose history
in regard to women we have briefly indicated,
double currents have been setting—one upwards
and the other down. While the capacity of
women has been rising, the political dignity of
men has been falling, year by year.

Small need to recapitulate the successive
stages of this fall. Every one knows how the
franchise of the antique republics, at last extended to all the male inhabitants of the commonwealth except the slaves, was practically
annihilated with the establishment of the
Roman Empire, and how Charlemagne, late in
the ninth century, sought to recall the extinct
breath of antique liberty by initiating representative assemblies. Representation grafted a

fertile modern idea upon the direct popular franchise, which alone was known to antiquity.

In all Anglo-Saxon communities, whether in their Germanic homes or in England, self-government appears at the very dawn of history. Among the Teutons, the affairs of the "mark-moot," the "hundred," and the state assembly were conducted by all the freemen of the tribe. In the deliberation of the assembled people, every man had an equal voice; and it was the custom for all to appear fully armed. * After the Saxon conquest of Britain, the primitive Teutonic village community represented a settlement made up of eorls or nobles, ceorls or simple freemen, landless men or laets, and finally slaves. The two first classes alone possessed land, and in virtue of that possession were alone entitled to political rights. In the "tun-moot," or primitive township, which elected its own officers and provided for the representation of its interests in the courts of the hundred and the shire, appears the earliest English form of the representative principle.

From the eorls and ceorls developed the entire body of English freemen—on the one hand the nobility, the thanes; on the other the yeo-

* Tacitus, *Germania.*

manry and untitled but land-owning commoners. All the political life of England has been
carried on by these two classes, alone articulate
in history, and so much so that it is easy to suppose that no other class existed, and that political rights were universal. But it is estimated
that at the time of the Norman Conquest two
thirds of the people of England belonged to the
unrepresented class of serfs and slaves.

" The runaway slave could be flogged, or, *if a woman*,
burned to death." *

All women were similarly deprived either of
the right to assemble in the primary caucus or
town-meetings, or of a voice in the selection of
representatives for the shire. But if in this
political privation they shared the destiny of the
" unfree," of the laets and slaves, and of the
debtors, criminals, foreigners, captives and pris-
oners of war, by which these luckless classes
were constantly being recruited, the women of
the higher classes at least were partially compensated by sharing the special social consideration accorded to the men of their own order.
What is of more importance for our present
purpose, the idea that women could share any

* Green, *Short History of the English People*, vol. i., p. 28.

other consideration had as yet occurred to no-
body. Into a meeting of armed men, it would
have seemed absurd for women to intrude; and
the questions raised at these primitive assemblies
were too simply and exclusively connected with
the " provision and defence " of the community
to suggest any advantage to be derived from the
counsels of women.

When the general assembly of the tribe had
shrunk to the aristocratic witenagemot of the
heptarchy—the selected councillors of the king,
the germ of the future House of Lords; when
under Henry II. the National Council, prothal-
tus of the House of Commons, was definitely
organized, and summons issued regularly to
archbishops, bishops, abbots, priors, earls,
barons, knights, and freeholders*—women were
still excluded, for the reason that they had
never before been admitted. At this period,
by the thirteenth century, and thence onwards,
society had become sufficiently complex, sufficiently removed from the original nucleus of
exclusive concern for " provision and defence,"
to have furnished many of the intrinsic reasons
for woman suffrage which exist to-day. But

* *Origin and Growth cf English Constitution*, Hannis Taylor,
1889, p. 289.

memory of the primitive past still dominated
the actual time : the "dead man's mailed
hand" here, as in so many other directions, still
weighed heavily enough to control the situation.

The evolution of the situation illustrated the
proverb : who goes not forward, goes back.
Women did not only fail to participate in the
growing rights of national representation, but
they lost the feudal rights of individual petty
sovereignty, which many women in the upper
classes had formerly possessed.

"The condition of the landed estate predomi-
nated over the condition of the person, so that
the woman who held the fief had all the privileges of the noble, vassal, or rather all the
rights of sovereignty : right to raise troops, coin
money, administer civil and criminal justice.
Her right in these respects was as absolute as
that of men. But these great rights of noble
women were gradually extinguished during the
fourteenth century." *

In characteristic agreement with the method
of dealing with the rights of women which has
generally prevailed, one right was saved for
them in the midst of this general lapse : in de-

---

* Laboulaye, *Recherches sur la Condition Civil et Politique des
Femmes,—Memoir Couronné*, 1842, p. 442.

fault of male heirs, baronies were allowed to descend to baronial heiresses, "who, although they could not themselves sit in the king's council, conveyed to their husbands the presumptive right to receive his summons." *

"The husbands even continued to sit after the death of their wives as tenants by the curtesy." †

This custom, like a fashion designed for velvet, which reproduces itself in fustian and calico, subsequently extended from baronial fiefs to the property of commoners, so that every husband, though he might not sit in the king's council, could still be "tenant by curtesy" of the inheritance of his wife.

During this same thirteenth century, the national assembly assumed a new type: that of the "estate system," in which three classes or orders of society, definitely established as clergy, baronage, and commons, appeared in person or by representatives. From that moment disappeared the last chance, had it ever existed, for women to appear in such assemblies, or to have a voice in choosing representatives to them. The Assembly was intended to represent not individuals, but orders, estates; and it

* Taylor, *loc. cit.*, p. 436.   † Hallam, vol. iii., p. 119.

was plausible to assume that women were adequately represented by the men of their own
order ; or, when they belonged to unrepresented
classes, that women should share the political
exclusion of their men. This theory dominated
the entire system of English political thought
for six centuries, even beyond the moment of the
great Reform Bill of 1832. For that bill was
not planned to secure wider individual representation—a plan which could hardly have been
practically devised previous to the Revolution
of 1848. The reform was simply intended to
rectify abuses occurring in borough and other
class representation, abuses which had grown
up, not through perversions of principle, but
through lapses of situation and changes of fact.

Before the fifteenth century, when the Parliament touched its first culminating point, women
had completely disappeared below the horizon
of public life. Coincidently, soon after this great
epoch, the liberties and prosperity of England
began to decline, and the condition of the people
to enter upon that insidious process of deteriora-
tion which was not to be arrested for more than
two centuries. When the lowest point of material and political degradation, for the mass of the
people, had been reached at the beginning of

the eighteenth century, the reaction set in ; and by 1848, not only popular, but universal suffrage had been established in France and in the United States. Then came the civil war, and at a bound, with a single stroke of the pen, the emancipated slaves were endowed with equal political rights. The farthest possible limit of the franchise for men was then reached. For the first time in the history of the world, all the women of the State were rendered the political inferiors of all the men in it and so remain. No matter how well born, how intelligent, how highly educated, how virtuous, how rich, how refined, the women of to-day constitute a political class below that of every man, no matter how base born, how stupid, how ignorant, how vicious, how poverty-stricken, how brutal. The pauper in the almshouse may vote ; the lady who devotes her philanthropic thought to making that almshouse habitable, may not. The tramp who begs cold victuals in the kitchen may vote ; the heiress who feeds him and endows universities may not. The half civilized hordes pouring into our country through the open gates of our seaport towns, the Indian if settled in severalty, the negro on the cotton plantation,—all, now, or in a few years, have a vote. But the white woman

of purest blood, and who, in her own person, or
that of mother or grandmother, has helped to
sustain the courage of the Revolutionary war, to
fight the heroic battle of abolition, and to dress
the wounds of the Rebellion,—this woman must
keep silence. Legislatures are .distracted by
controversies over the means to secure the
"illiterate vote"; pasters are provided, and
symbols; and in the meanwhile, all the women
—who embrace half the education, half the
virtue, and but a fraction of the illiteracy or
crime of the community—remain excluded from
the franchise, buried behind this dense cloud of
often besotted ignorance.

The above observations were made in the
address delivered before the Convention at the
New York hearing May 31, 1894 (see Appendix,
p. 210). On June 2d the following passages
appeared in an editorial of the *Evening Post.*

"One great cause of the woman-suffrage agitation is
the eagerness with which democracy has taken hold of
the machinery of government. . . . The work of government, which is, or ought to be, really a means only
towards human enjoyment and convenience, has come
to be considered one of the great ends of human existence. . . . The inordinate importance attached to
the business of governing, and the discredit heaped
on everybody who did not take part in it, have had

the effect of filling the minds of men and women with the idea that anybody who did not share in it was robbed of a natural right bestowed on him or her by the Creator.   To this we owe the indiscriminate distribution of the suffrage among all classes and conditions of males in all democratic countries, and the growing disregard of intelligence and character in admitting people to a share in the management of public affairs.   Nothing but a feeling that each person held his right to the franchise by the same title as his right to liberty or property, could have caused or excused the tremendous rush of barbarous men into the work of government during the past fifty years.   It was not unnatural that the women, seeing this, and hearing on all sides that electing people to office was one of the chief ends of man, and about the noblest work in which he could engage, should have begun to complain of their exclusion, and demand a fair share of what men made so much of."

The author of the present pamphlet may be

"Who the author of this production is, is wholly unnecessary to the public."

pardoned for a certain feeling of self-complacency, that the *Evening Post* thus condescended, in its editorial columns, to reply to the argument of a public address, which its columns of ordinary news had left entirely unnoticed. We trust the *Post* would not consider disrespectful the remark that, to the feminine ear, this reply bears a marvellous resemblance to those conscious sophisms of the nursery, wherewith tender mothers try to persuade their obstreperous children to desist from snatching at the fragile bric-a-brac which may have dazzled infantile fancy. "No, no, Tommy, don't touch that; it will hurt Tommy's pretty little hand; see, it cuts mamma; it is an ugly thing anyhow; mamma won't have it standing there to bother Tommy; here, nurse, come and take it away and throw it out of the window; dear mamma does not *want* Tommy to play with such an ugly old thing!" To whom comes, discreet, the nurse, conveys away under her apron the discredited bauble; until such time as the child's attention may have become sufficiently distracted by its own playthings, to permit the replacement of the contested toy in its old place of honor.

For that a place of honor, and none else, must be held by that in human society which is conspicuous, foremost, supreme in its own sphere, and which, in any sense, controls the actions and determines the status of all the members of society, no one knows better than the *Evening Post*. None better, than that the honor paid to government is not a fancy of the "French Rousseauites,"* nor of Democracy, and that the

* After all, only Robespierre was distinctly a disciple of Rousseau.

Evening Post approximates strangely towards the "anarchist idea" it condemns, in pretending, at least in this *argumentum ad foeminam*, that "government" is a matter of no consequence anyhow. But if this be the case, why object to the "rush of barbarous men" into it? Why should not all cultivated and refined people of both sexes content themselves with the reflection, that government is only a convenience, that intellectual pursuits are more dignified than politics, that afternoon teas are more elegant assemblages than primaries, that the ideas that mould public opinion in the long run are greater than the precepts that govern public actions at short range, that the pure science of the laboratory is of far more real importance than the applied science of the *Weekly Tribune*, that Goethe pronounced the speculations of Lamarck of far more consequence than the whole French Revolution, that Aristotle was really greater than Alexander, and Bacon and Shakespeare than Elizabeth, and that it is a more agreeable and humane way to spend one's evenings at home in perusal of the *Evening Post*, than to shout oneself hoarse either on the platform or in the audience of mass-meetings collected to influence the decisions of this low-down, no account, in-

convenient convenience of a democratic government!

Why? unless because, as Aristotle himself
remarked, even from the midst of his natural-
history museum, and surrounded by the exotic
gifts of Alexander, "Man is a political animal!"

At the moment the idea of Representation
was born into the world, came with it a twin, but
so imperfectly developed, so meagre and insignificant in appearance, it failed for ages to attract
any particular attention. This twin idea is, that
in a highly organized society, in a properly developed social organism, the function of government has become, if it never were before, twofold
—not only to rule, but to represent. To give,
and with constantly increasing definiteness, precision and efficiency, articulate expression to all
the forces, needs, interests, wills, and thoughts of
all the elements of the body politic, which thus,
and thus only, become fully, because thus only
socially, alive. The conception of the spiritual
and secular arm, distinctly enunciated so long ago
in the Roman state, and since dominating European history, has, like most powerful social con-
ceptions, a profound physiological basis and anal-
ogy. This conception for the social organism,
bases itself, though unconsciously, on the fact

that in the individual organism the brain is at once the organ of thought, and the organ of the will, which executes the purpose of thought. Further, that the thoughts generated during the processes of the brain, reflect innumerable vital actions sustained throughout the body, even to its extreme periphery, and whose influence, irradiated to the brain, initiates these same brain processes. One of the latest dicta of neurological science is, that in the mosaic of the brain cortex, the entire body is represented.

Although the representative function of government only began to be distinctly recognized when our Saxon ancestors began to send delegates from their "tun-moot" to their "hundred" and "shire"; yet in a vague but still most impressive way, the function of representation was discerned even in the Oriental monarchies which greet us at the dawn of history. To this was due the very majesty of the great king,—of Rameses, of Nebuchadnezzar, of Xerxes. In his personality was mysteriously concentrated all the personalities of vast empires—Scythian, Bactrian, Assyrian, Elamite, Arab, Copt.; Nineveh, Babylon, Susa, Thebes, and Memphis,—all fused together, until a tremendous quintessence of vital force could be distilled through the body and soul of the man, whose physical organs bore a superficial resemblance to those of the slave who stood behind the throne. Hence this physical appearance was rejected as an illusion of sense—just as in later ages devout Catholics rejected the physical aspect of the blessed bread and wine, and saw in these the veritable body and blood of Christ.

To a properly developed social imagination, the social organs, through whose medium is manifested the collective force and vital action of a great people, should be invested with no less sublime dignity than that which humanity has always, (and not only since New York began to hold parlor meetings for suffrage) invested its rulers and kings. We are in a period of temporary eclipse of faith; and so content to despise indiscriminately, our symbols, our rulers, and even the representatives of ourselves. But man lives by faith and cannot long live without it.

At present, the view of government which the *Evening Post* (but only for the present purpose) advocates, leads directly to many of the very evils which the *Evening Post* is constantly expending most strenuous energies to combat. Because the idea of sovereignty has become detached from all previously admitted attributes of sovereignty, is no longer necessarily associated with any insignia of intrinsic power, the conception of sovereignty itself has become lax, feeble, confused.

Sovereignty, divided into a million fragments, seems illusory, worthless. "Absurd," women are told, "to struggle for the right of suffrage, when that means nothing. You might as well pine for the privilege of riding in a crowded omnibus, when you already have the right of driving in your comfortable carriage. The right to rule yourselves! No one rules himself, much less any one else. What personal influence may be exerted by tongue or pen, can be done by the unenfranchised full as well as by those who possess the illusory privilege of the ballot. I, who am legally entitled to vote, do not vote half the time. What, then, do you want to vote for?"

"No one rules!" Yet, according to the dictum of a master in political thought, the first question to be decided in any community is: Where rests the Sovereign Power? The answer, according to the theory of a democratic society, is: With Public Opinion. According to the theory of a Republic, the sovereignty lies, with such Public Opinion as shall prove itself, through superior virtue and intelligence, to be not only the best, but the strongest. For intelligence must be stronger than ignorance, and virtue than vice, wherever free play is really allowed to each.

This is the answer according to theory. The answer according to fact must be that the Sovereign Power rests upon physical force. Otherwise it would be incomprehensible that Power, thus defined, should remain confined to the sex whose only universal superiority lay in physical force; and that the sex which admittedly possessed in abundance the attributes of intelligence and virtue should be excluded from all share in the Sovereign Power.

This cynical answer has indeed been given; given, *mirabile dictu*, even by clergymen, by those whose profession dictates the constant exaltation of mental over physical qualification for the Sovereignty.

Nevertheless, not only the answer is not true, but, what is more important for our purpose, no one really believes that in modern societies it is true. Every one knows that physical force is at present the servant, and not, if it has ever been, the master of intelligence. If, with the advent of manhood suffrage, apparently unintelligent masses often obtain supreme control, it can only be because intelligence has either abdicated or declined. The control is not at all due to the possession of a vast amount of latent physical force, which by itself is as useless as the river, which is as yet unturned into the mill race.

Who abdicates, but those who call the privilege of the ballot illusory?

The complex contradictions in the present distributions of Sovereign Power are further intensified by the vulgarization of the general ideal. It is one thing to say, "Some men shall rule," quite another to declare, "All men shall rule," and that in virtue of the most primitive, the most rudimentary attribute they possess, that namely of sex. If the original contempt for masses of men has ever diminished, and the conception of mankind been ennobled, it is because, upon the primitive animal foundation, human imagination has built a fair structure of mental and moral attribute and possibility, and habitually deals with that. This indeed is no new thing to do; for it was to this moral man that Pericles addressed his funeral oration; and of whom Lincoln thought in his speech at Gettysburg.

Of this moral man, women—the sex hitherto

so despised—are now recognized to constitute an integral part. It is useless therefore to attempt to throw them out by an appeal to the primitive conditions of a physical force, to which no one appeals for any other purpose.

It is forgotten to-day that, until to-day, the incapacity of women for the suffrage was attributed, not merely to their deficiency in physical force, but to the profound mental and moral inferiority of her entire nature. Whether this theory was ultimately derived from the natural contempt of the primitive savage for every one whom he could knock down; or whether, as the Canon Law asserts, it is the natural punishment for the seduction of Adam by Eve, and the expression of the subsequent natural indignation of the human race, which owes to the same fact its existence and its fall; certain it is that this theory has prevailed throughout Christendom down to the second half of the nineteenth century, and is only just beginning to wane in its force and in its extraordinary practical efficiency.

During the long ages of class rule, which are just beginning to cease, only one form of sovereignty has been assigned to all men—that, namely, over all women. Upon these feeble and inferior companions all men were permitted to avenge the indignities they suffered from so many men to whom they were forced to submit. To-day, when all men rule, and diffused self-government has abolished the old divisions between the governing classes and the governed, only one class remains over whom all men can exercise sovereignty—namely, the women. Hence a shuddering dread runs through society at the proposal to also abolish this last refuge of facile domination.

"Shall man make over to woman half of the sovereign power which has hitherto been his, and which, if he chooses, he can keep? . . . It is incumbent on the present holders of power, before abdicating, to consider whether in the common interest their abdication is to be desired."*

Mr. Goldwin Smith, like Mr. Francis Parkman, writes as an historian, a closet student, easily affected by abstract terms and general ideas. In these pages we ourselves have also greatly affected general ideas; and have enunciated a claim to a share in the sovereignty, in very much the same spirit as Mr. Smith urges men not to "abdicate." Let us, however, now

* Goldwin Smith, *Woman Suffrage. Essays on Questions of the Day*, 1893.

descend, where neither of these eminent his-
torians really ever deigns to descend, into the
arena of practical issues and daily life, and
inquire in what sense men would "abdicate
their sovereignty" if women also voted.

Whether we take a township of a thousand
voters electing a school commissioner, or a city
electing its mayor, or the whole country voting
for President,—the principle is the same; so we
may keep to the convenience of the smaller
numbers.

Suppose when the men had voted alone, 300
had decided for candidate A, and 700 for B,
who was therefore elected. On the next occasion, say in 1895, a thousand women had, in
the same locality, been added to the electorate.
The 700 men, plus 500 women, vote on this
occasion for B; 300 men and 500 women vote
for A. As before, B is elected, and the 700
men, in the second case as in the first, secure
their choice. In what way then could they be
said to have "abdicated the sovereignty?"

Take another combination. In a third election 700 of the women unite with the 700 men;
and the combination, being the majority, again
carries its candidate, only more women have the
satisfaction of succeeding than when they had

divided equally between the successful and the unsuccessful parties. In another possibility, 800 women might unite with only 400, or even 300 men, and the 1100 total would be victorious over the remaining 900 of the electorate, where the beaten party would contain a majority of the male voters (700), and a minority of the female (200). This is the occasion so much dreaded, in which the men would seem to have been overpowered by a female vote.

Evidently the occasion would only recur from time to time, among the infinite number of possible combinations, and could no more be considered the rule than a throw of double sixes on dice. And when it does occur, where is the harm? Why the anticipation of such insufferable humiliation at this special combination of persons? This would not be avowed if the thousand new voters added to the town were Swedes, as might be the case in Wisconsin; or Hungarians, as in some mining settlement of Pennsylvania; or Irish, as easily happens in New York. There is only one supposition that can explain the sentiment of horror which the mere suggestion of this occasional electoral combination undoubtedly inspires many people: it is that they have not learned to think of

women as *persons*. The addition of their vote
does not seem to them the addition of so many
more hundred or thousand people to the voting
list; but of a "feminine element," an incalculable
quantity, something unknown, mysterious, and
with which, at all events, it would be horribly
"unmanly" to be associated. Like the valiant
husband retreated under the bed, the representative of this class of thinkers declares, "While
I have the spirit of a man in me, I will not
come out and submit to this outrage!"

But, from the moment that women have been
made persons before the law, it is illegal to
treat them otherwise. It is really a breach of
the law to depress them from the status of so
many other people, to that of vague elemental
forces.

Nevertheless, this is done all the time. Reformers, deeply concerned for minority representation, as is just, and bewailing the crudities
of representative government in its infancy,
dwell on the woes of the democrats who never
get heard in Vermont, and of the republicans
who are silenced in South Carolina. But for
the women who may not be heard anywhere,
and who, forbidden to speak, cease in innumerable directions to know how to think,—for

these the sensitive reformers feel neither sympathy nor concern. And why? Because women are not to them persons.

It may be said, for it has been said, that the objection to seeing a vote of 700 men overcome by a coalition of 300 men with 800 women, lies in the fact that the defeated minority knows, if it had a free hand and was allowed to use fisticuffs, it could pound into a jelly a majority composed so largely of women. It would feel, therefore, sullen, restive, and justly indignant, that it should be prohibited from using this power and obliged to submit to a merely nominal force and supremacy. For "there is no force behind the votes of women."

But is it only in such an hypothetical case that a minority would know it could, if allowed to resort to physical force, shiver to fragments the majority? The burly brakeman in railroad strikes would probably, in a fair hand-to-hand encounter, be much bested over all the stockholders of the road,—weakened, not only because they included women in their midst, but also by sedentary habits and predominantly indoor occupations. Why do they not try this way of settling their difficulties? Why do not the classes in England who still remain entirely un-

represented, but with whom rests so much physical strength, drop their fists into the balance,
as Brennus his sword, and cut short the futile,
womanish, discussion?

The answer is really in every one's mouth. It
is not that it cannot be done, but that, on the
whole, people are all agreed that it is best it
should not be done. It is not that physical
force is respected less, but that mental force
is respected more. Once the feudal baron, unable to sign his name, laughed at the swordless
clerk. To-day the laugh has changed, and
while it is permissible not to be a skilled ath-
lete, it is everywhere considered a disgrace to
sign with a mark, everywhere, that is, except
when exercising the functions of popular sovereignty at the polls.

We note these things not because we ourselves
have any dislike for fighting, or any contempt for
physical force, or any belief that in its absence,
and in default of the joyous courage born of
tense muscles and well knit bones, any State
could survive. But merely because, in the natural development of societies from primitive beginnings to modern complexities, many things
have been added to the primitive nucleus; and
these complicate all decisions, and transfer the

idea of power to many other forces besides those which inspire a blow.

It is not, therefore, "abdication of sovereignty" which is proposed, demanded, or to be dreaded in extending the suffrage to women. It is simply the association of women with men, for such functions of sovereignty as they are able to exercise, and whose dissociation from some others has for precedent a similar dissociation among the functions of the complex modern State.

"One of the features of a revolutionary era is the prevalence of a feeble facility of abdication. The holders of power, however natural and legitimate it may be, are too ready to resign it on the first demand. . . . The nerves of authority are shaken by the failure of conviction." *

* Goldwin Smith, *loc. cit.*, p. 185.

V.

MR. SMITH cannot be said to fail to show how the admission of women to the electorate would cause the "abdication" of men, for he does not even try. Rather does he jump about with grave excitement from one point to another, mixing many things, all accessible things, together, until he has concocted a veritable *olla podrida,* a *potpourri* of an argument, whose details are a wonderful collection of unrelated parts. The problem offered is to show why, in a representative system based on the double principle that all the intelligence in the State shall be enlisted for its welfare, and all the weakness in the State represented for its own defence, women, being often intelligent, often weak, and always persons in the community, should not also be represented. To show that they should not, Mr. Smith tells us: "That sexual revolution must have its limitation if the human race is to continue." "That the movement in favor of

93

woman suffrage is part of a general attempt to change the relations between the sexes." "That laws passed by the woman's vote will be felt to have no force behind them." "That the transfer of power from the military to the unmilitary sex involves national emasculation." "That a man who prized his home would protest against any proposal to give the family more than one vote." "That women are not a class but a sex, with class interests throughout the scale identical with those of the man,— and effectually represented by the male vote." "That women as a sex have no wrongs which male legislatures cannot be expected to redress, so it is not necessary, to obtain redress, that there shall be an abdication by man of the sovereign power." "That women are (unfortunately) already admitted to professions of medicine, law, and teaching; to male universities, to government clerkships, thus depriving of a place many worthy men who would otherwise support them in marriage." "That if some women are underpaid, time will redress the injustice, which after all is not extensive, since a needlewoman has a light trade and could not be paid like a stevedore, and the gains of prima donnas are enormous." "That punishment for marital infi-

delity must be more severe on the woman because she brings an adulterine child into the
family." "That unenfranchised women are not
nearly as ill off as were American slaves."
"That wife-beating is sometimes justified by the
unspared husband-nagging which had preceded
it." "That divorce should not be made too
easy." "That marriage is a restraint imposed
on the passions of the man for the benefit of
the woman, . . . and woman would not be
benefited by its abolition." "That Shelley
was a brute to Harriet, and Mr. Mill infatuated
by his hallucination about the surpassing genius
of Mrs. Mill." "That in the earliest stages of
civilization the family was socially, legally, and
politically a unit." "That Mill's calm nature is
betrayed into violence in his denunciation of the
present institution of marriage, . . . and no
woman could regard with complacency a female
spiritualist installed beside her hearth." "That
some of the champions of women aim to make
them independent of marriage." "That a passion
for emulating the male sex has taken possession
of some women, as women under the Roman Em-
peror began to play the gladiator when other
excitements were exhausted." "That women
cannot be both the helpmate and complement

of man, and at the same time his rival and competitor." "That writing Greek or Latin has not been very useful to the generality of male students, and would be therefore useless to women." "That St. Paul ratifies the unity of the family, the authority of its head, and the female need of that headship." "In this movement of sexual revolution, the family is practically threatened with dissolution." "Woman, if she becomes a man, will be a weaker man,—yet must be prepared to resign her privileges as a woman." "In an age of flabby sentiment and servile worship of change, we have had enough of weak and precipitate abdications. To one of them we owe the catastrophe of the French revolution."

At this catastrophe, as a good place to stop, let us draw breath. We have cited Mr. Smith's arguments running, but exactly in the order in which he presents them, and nearly always in his exact words. These multifarious statements may be good; they may be warranted; they may show just such a range of miscellaneous information as is to be expected from a writer and professor of history; they may have all the philosophic calm from which Mill was betrayed, and all the poetic fervor which failed to exon-

erate Shelley; but in the name of all the
syllogisms of logic, what have they to do with
the case? Not the flowers which bloom in
the spring, tra-la, would seem to be more
irrelevant.

Mr. Smith observes that Mr. Mill's writings
on the subjection of women are to be studied in
the light afforded by his autobiography. Similarly, in estimating this remarkable contribution
to the questions of the day, it is fair to remember the vehemence with which Mr. Smith has
written against the principle of Home Rule for
Ireland; and the fact that, though professor of
history at Cornell, he is reported to have had
nothing but sneers for the admission of women
students to his classes. Mr. Smith does not
come to the discussion of the Political Rights of
Women with a cool and unbiassed mind. But,
as no one else does, nor perhaps can, this is
hardly a reproach.

It is noticeable that, throughout the diatribe
—for it is this rather than a discussion,—Mr.
Smith brings no political reasons to bear on a
question of political right. He does not even
note the special incongruity of the admission to
the legal profession of women who are still des-
titute of political rights and of any share in the

government of the country.   He plants himself
squarely on the basis of Sex Instinct.   He talks
exactly like the blustering husband (how many
thousands of them there are !), who declares his
wife's expression of opinion in regard to Tommy's schooling or the behavior of the coachman,
an invasion of his own prerogative as head of
the house.   The comparison is most literal, for
over and over again through the essay does Mr.
Smith affirm, that to permit women to express,
through the ballot, their opinion in regard to
the management of schools, or the behavior of
officials, is to demand that " man hand over the
government to her," (p. 218).   Under the in-
spiration of a (possibly recent) perusal of
Taine's *Ancien Régime*, Mr. Smith sees, in the
willingness of American men to consider fairly
this new application of the principles of democratic government, only a repetition of the fatu-
ous cowardice with which French noblemen
handed over their chateaus to a Revolutionary
mob.

Reading these solemn references to sex relations, and marriage, and adultery, and divorce,
and Shelley, and Roman gladiators, it is difficult
to escape a feeling of bewilderment, almost of
vertigo.   Do sex relations depend upon acts of

Parliament or constitutional amendments ? Can
women marry a ballot, or embrace the franchise,
otherwise than by a questionable figure of
speech ? Must adultery and infanticide necessarily be favored by the decisions of female
jurors ? Is divorce legislation, as arranged by
the exclusive wisdom of men, now so satisfactory,
that women—who must perforce be involved in
every case—should always modestly refrain
from attempting amendment ?

This entire class of considerations, however
irrelevant to the issue, may be grouped together,
and considered together, because, to a large
class of minds—the rudest, quite as much as
those of Mr. Smith's cultivation—they are the
considerations which do come to the front
whenever Equal Rights are suggested.

The reason is that men, accustomed to think
of men as possessing sex attributes and other
things besides, are accustomed to think of
women as having sex, and nothing else. Against
this immense and insolent assumption, it is true
that the women of this century, and most emphatically the women of this latter half of it,
have revolted. Their demand for equality does
not mean a claim to be considered equal in
power or achievement, except or until facts may,

in the individual cases, demonstrate such equality. No one imagines that, by voting, the female
industrial, who does less work, can secure the
same pay as the man who does more ; but only
that, indirectly, but soon, she will secure equal
pay when she does the same work, and better
pay when she does better,—which is not now
the case. No one believes that, through exercise
of the franchise, the female teacher, physician,
artist, or writer, will be made the equal of their
male compeers, whenever they cannot approximate to them by other agencies. It would not
even be supposed possible that the act of casting a vote in New York would, of itself, enable
a female essayist to compete with Mr. Smith in
Toronto. But what is imagined, claimed, and
very seriously demanded, is, that women be
recognized as human beings, with a range of
faculties and activities co-extensive with that of
men, whatever may be the difference in the
powers within this range. The sex relations of
women as lovers, as wives, as mothers, remain
absolutely untouched, certainly unimpaired, by
the demand to extend beyond these. What is
impaired, is not the sex relation nor sex condition, but the social disabilities, the personal
and social subordination, the condition of

political non-existence, which have been foisted upon that sex condition. Because the strength of the wife is on the average less than that of the husband, it does not follow that it is in-decorous for a wife to sit down to eat ₊at the same table with her husband. Yet that until rather recently was the custom among the peasantry of Central Europe. Because the father of a child owes protection to its mother, and both are morally bound to be faithful in the marriage bond, is not a reason to assert that the wife and daughters in a family should have no voice in public affairs, while husband and sons had. Because Mrs. Smith is (we hope) a help-meet, comfort, and complement to Mr. Smith, it does not follow that she may not be a rival and competitor with Mr. Jones. Indeed, arguing on general principles, we should suppose that Mr. Smith would, *in re* Jones, prefer that situation rather than the other one. In modern times, and outside of Oneida Communities, it is usually ex-pected that a woman's relations with her hus-band should not be the type of, but the em-phatic contrast to, her relations with every other man. If not, how can marriage be such a " beneficial restraint " as Mr. Smith declares it to be ? But if this be the case, what is the use of

talking about marriage, when we are talking
about voting? Do all the men who "prize
their homes" insist that the whole family shall
have only one opinion? But if multiple opinions, why not multiple votes? Ah, because, re-
plies Mr. Smith (we presume), a discussion over
a breakfast table is harmless—it leads to nothing. Romola may call Tito a treacherous man,
but he retains the whip hand, and reminds her,
"the envoys are gone, the library sold, and you
are my wife." But a vote is an efficient force,
it tends to accomplish something. That may
be something I don't like; imagine, then, the
humiliation of seeing that brought about by a
woman! There it is again—the humiliation!
If one thousand men vote against me, I submit,
and bide my turn; but if seven hundred men
and three hundred women carry a measure, it is
intolerable. "Laws passed by the woman's
vote would be felt to have no force behind
them." Not even the force of all the men who
agreed with them or with whom they agreed?
But if effective assertion of female opinion in
public—possibly remote—affairs be so galling
to the masculine pride of the men who "prize
their homes," how have they been able to tolerate the loss of the practical domestic sovereignty

whose delights were so much more tangible and
appreciable? "One thing is not French," said
Napoleon—"that a woman should do as she
pleases." But nowadays she does pretty much
as she pleases, yet men do not seem ill content.
A woman comes and goes to her own house,
and, in New York State at least, her husband
does not suspect her of a rendezvous, even if she
be occasionally late to dinner. She is not forbidden to learn to read and write lest she correspond with lovers; she is not restricted to any
household employment she can contrive to get
any one else to carry on for her; she can go to
college though unmarried, and though married
she may make a will; she can select her own
church, and defy her husband's sentiments on
infant baptism; she can keep her own check-
book, no matter whence she obtains her funds,
from father, husband, or her own exertions; she
can occupy her own time in her own way, think
her own thoughts, express her own wishes,
carry out her own plans—indeed, do such a
number of things all out of her own head as
must be perfectly maddening to the scholars
deeply impressed with the "female need of
headship." *O tempora! O mores!* Times have
changed, and we with them.

"Quem enim Romanorum pudet uxorem ducere in convivium ? Aut cujus non mater-familias primum locum tenet ædium atque in celebritate versatur ? Quod multo fit aliter in Græcia." *

Can it be possible that Mr. Smith is unaware of this domestic revolution which has been thus effected under his very nose ? He does not complain of things as they are, but only as they might be ; he cannot, therefore, be anxious that domestic authority has already in any way declined. There are households whose female members have a way of getting their own way with marvellous facility by the simple process of never talking back to the tall talk of the master of the house. He does the talking and lays down the law—in the theory ; they attend to the practice. Is there some such occult reason lurking for Mr. Smith also among the *res angustas domi*, that he continues to imagine the dreadful time is coming, and does not see that it has already come? If he can tolerate the present freedom of thought and life which law, custom, and public opinion to-day secure to his wife and daughter, why does he feel so badly, so terribly, at a remote possibility that their vote should one day affect the selection of the Governor for

* Cornelius Nepos, Præfatio.

Canada, or be counted in among the agencies which should decide the foreign policy for Hawaii? If the shoe does not pinch, why should the mantle?

If the "transfer of power from the military to the unmilitary sex involve national emasculation," and the right to representation implies such "transfer of power," how can a peaceful historian venture to vote? Who proposes to "transfer" anything? The big boy is on the sofa, the little sister uncomfortably on the ground. Because after a while she clambers to a seat, and persuades him to resist his primitive manly impulse to kick her down, it does not follow that *he* is displaced. If a youth and a maiden walking through a field are attacked by a bull, it is not customary to suppose that her presence will compel him to run away. It is rather expected it would act as an additional incentive, if needs be, to make him fight.

This idea that masculine work cannot proceed if there is any woman around ; or that, though she may be innocuous while looking on, she must fatally "lower the standard" if she takes a hand at it herself, is very funny but very old. It has, indeed, an air of venerable senility. In the last fifty years how often it has been de-

clared, with all the pathos of menaced vested
interests, that even the diplomas already conferred upon men would become worthless were
women subsequently admitted to the learned
institution which had conferred them. If men
cannot maintain their standard in war or learning, or anything else, when the women speak,
why is it so much easier when they are silent,
yet stay around pretty much the same? Mr.
Smith and many others seem to imagine that a
boy studies his Latin lesson in one way if he is
all alone in a room, in another way if a girl sits
down with her dictionary at the other side of
the table ; that the farmers' sons at Cornell
will show depth of thought over their historical
lectures while shut up with each other, but only
"shallow quickness" if contaminated by the
presence of girls. Women cannot take up an
occupation, they can only "invade a sphere."
Their passion for emulating the male sex is
such that they are threatening to deprive some
energetic members of it of their surest chance
of making a living by getting possession of
government clerkships. Roman women, if
Juvenal be correct, fought as gladiators.
American women, if Goldwin Smith be well
informed, count Treasury notes, and are thus

made independent of marriage. In the meanwhile, the friend * of poor women, who secured
them this avenue of employment, purposely
kept their salaries low, that men with votes
should not be tempted to claim their places.

In a general upheaval the things which were
at the bottom come up to the top. It is only
in moments of radical discussion like the present, and when the possibility of a practical issue
excites the expectation and the temper, that
the really ugly facts and beliefs—whose atmosphere, unacknowledged, is affecting everybody
all the time—are brought distinctly into view.
It is then possible for a writer who ought to
know better, to denounce the thoroughly Anglo-
Saxon movement for the extension of equal
rights as a " sexual revolution threatening the
family with dissolution, and turning woman
into a weaker man."

This is equivalent to admitting that it is
owing to the great predominance of purely sex
ideas about women that they have hitherto
been restricted to unequal rights. That families
cannot be held together on any basis of inter-
familial justice, equality, affection, and fundamental instinct, but must dissolve, not when the

* General Spinner.

Patria Potestas ceases, but when the recognized equality of women begins. That the " differentiation of the sexes," which lends such a charm to life, merely means the permanent maintenance of such inequality of horizon and opportunity as shall always leave women at some disadvantage, provide that they are always less well equipped for their work, and less well paid, and increase the chances that this work will always be rather less well done. That yet the differences between men and women are so small that they will entirely disappear the instant the one great difference of position is abolished, whereby men in private or in public are always expected to order, bully, or command; the women always to submit, shrink, and obey. The pleasure of life will be gone when there is no one left to boss! All the feminine charm, all the womanly grace, all the bewitchment, all the dear delight, that from the beginning of time men have been ascribing to women, does not lie in them, but outside of them; it is not a potency, it is a situation; it is not a natural force, it is a political contrivance; it has not been celebrated in poetry and song because men love women, but only because men love to order women around! What a mournful disillusion!

Are there, however, no real and serious objections to woman suffrage ? It is impossible to take Mr. Smith seriously. But in the discussions which have animated New York during these April days,

"Their flag to April's breeze unfurled,"

serious and fair-minded men have occasionally brought forward considerations, which serve at least to explain the historic situation ; the long exclusion of women from political rights; and the bewildered hesitation now felt when they claim them.

The following concise statement briefly sums up the argument.*

"By division of labor between human mates, the centre of activity for the female is the nest, where she works, apart from other mated females, supreme unto herself as to the ways and means of her duties. For the male, however, the centre of activity is the common field where he works in industrial relation with his fellow-males.

"In gregarious animals generally this industrial relation between the males begets concert of action for mutual advantage.

* *The Philosophy of It.* Edward Curtis, M.D.—Private communication.

" With civilized man such concert of action takes the form of an association, wherein certain members are detailed to devise rules and regulations for the common weal of the workers; others, etc. . . . Such association grown from simple beginnings to the complex organization known as The State, is thus, primordially and essentially, an organization *of* the males, *by* the males, *for* the masculine function of provision and defence of the family. . . . Females cannot claim an equal voice in the affairs of such an organization on the plea of 'equal rights for all.'

"'Equal rights for all' ·is an ellipsis for equal rights in the same thing, for all the similarly conditioned as to the thing.

" Women never have to *defend*, and only are called upon to *provide* if they are in the abnormal condition of lacking or having lost a natural male protector.

" In the councils of the community's providers and defenders, the normally conditioned woman can have no right to any voice at all; and no claim for an impossible partial voice can be entered for the abnormal few.

" Nor yet on the ground of obvious benefit to the community: for (it would be absurd that)

men in the conduct of their self-imposed task
for the provision and defence of the family
should be obliged to abide as much by the
opinions of their female mates as their own :—
since these would be the opinions of the inexperienced, the irresponsible, and the organically
different."

Here is the whole thing in a nutshell. Men
support women, at least "in normal conditions,"
as an equivalent for the prehistoric service of
keeping off wild beasts, knocking down fellow-
men, and bringing home to the family roast
the toothsome antelope or succulent bear. All
public affairs, including the government which
supervises and defends them, develop from
the group of events which began to happen
outside the cave: all private affairs continue
the incidents that occurred within. The sex
line is drawn along eternal division of the Ins
and the Outs; only, to be accurate, the names
should usually be reversed, and the situation
turned outside-in.

Because the foregoing statement is most abstract in character, and philosophic in form, it
is not therefore a true presentation of existing
circumstances. To use the Comtean phrase,
while reasoning about men is now generally

sustained on a basis of positive thought, the reasoning about women scarcely ever emerges from the stage of theology or metaphysics. Mr. Goldwin Smith confounds into one abstract sex relation, the relations of a wife with her husband, of a female clerk with her employer, of a saleswoman with the dry-goods dealer, of a factory operative with the manufacturer, of a school teacher with the school board, of a pupil with her professor, of a student at a co-educational university with her fellow—in a word, all the conceivable social relations which might be established by any woman in the community, with any man in it. Similarly, though less crudely, Dr. Curtis substitutes a generalization of the facts of "nesting" and "mating," as observed in natural history, for the historic facts of human society. Like the antique theories about necessarily circular orbits of heavenly bodies, this generalization is entirely congruous with itself; but—with nothing else. Natural history, with all its limitations, stands at one end of this argument; but an indefinitely multiplied personal experience is at the other. In Dr. Curtis' *Philosophy of It*, this double standpoint is described with equal clearness and force. The concluding sentence seems to break out almost involuntarily from the depths of a very precious personal experience, and as such cannot fail to appeal to thousands who may be fortunate enough to share the like.

Still, a personal experience, though multiplied a thousand-fold, is not necessarily a philosophic generalization.

When we remember the thousands of men throughout the State who every morning leave their homes to go forth to their work until evening; who reap hay in the broiling sun; or guide the energies of mighty steam-engines; or plod through the mazes of intricate business; or who bear any of the multitudinous burdens of arduous, responsible, or monotonous toil: when we remember the visions that follow these men all day long, of wife and children at home, nested in cosy nooks, or rambling through pleasant places, sheltered, protected, provided for by the brain and arm which are laboring in their behalf—when we think of these things, and of the pictures of the situation which arise so readily to the mind at its suggestion, we may wonder much less at the influence which is, coincidently, usually drawn.

"Thy husband is thy lord, thy life, thy keeper,
Thy head, thy sovereign; one that cares for thee

7

> And for thy maintenance ; commits his body
> To painful labor, both by sea and land ;
> To watch the night in storms, the day in cold,
> Whilst thou liest warm at home, secure and safe."

Nevertheless, closer scrutiny will find flaws in this plausible theory—flaws at every angle. The audience who listened to Katherine's mischievous eloquence knew *its* flaw very well; Petruchio had come "to wive it wealthily in Padua ; " and an American public cannot easily forget that with us, either property earned or property inherited is no longer admitted to be the basis of representation.   This has been the English theory ; but it is not ours.

"Lord Palmerston said, that those who have no property ought not to be the persons to direct the legislation applicable to those who have property." *

"We no longer think it desirable to give political representation to wealth, or to anything but persons. We have become thoroughly democratic, but our great-grandfathers had not." †

The primitive savage claimed to "support his wife," and inserted a promise to do so in his marriage ceremony.   What he meant was that

* *Hansard's Debates*, vol. 153, col. 771.   Quoted by Cox, *English Reform Bills*, p. 16.
† Fiske, *Critical Period of American History*, p. 257.

he would bring home game for her to cook, and make garments out of the skins. He counted the hunting as work, and the cooking as mere play—a conception which the estimate of later ages has exactly reversed.

Considering that all the industries of the world have developed out of the household labors of women, it is an odd "philosophy" which assumes that women have been habitu- ally "supported" in idleness by men. From the virtuous woman of Solomon to Lydia, the merchant of Tyrian dye; from the guild mis- tresses of England to the factory girls of Low- ell, everywhere and always we find women at work. Their work has lacked formal social recognition, which is the very thing to-day com- plained of; it has been blotted out by such phrases as, "The man 'supports' his mate," and, "the male mates combine for provision and defence." But at most, and for the most time, obviously, the man has simply brought home to his wife the raw material for her industry.

Not for the first time to-day, but to-day un- questionably, and on a large scale, women have moreover crossed the threshold of the home— or "nest"—and entered the "gainful occupa- tions" classified in the census. As already

shown, there are in the United States to-day at
least three million women so classified, and in
1880, 360,000 of these were in the State of New
York. This is one eighth of the total female
population, as estimated in 1890.

In Europe 4,000,000 women are employed in factory
labor alone, and economists say, "we could not possibly
do without them."

Although no general statistics exist on the
civil status of women so engaged, Carroll
Wright's interesting researches in twenty cities
found among 17,000 working women 15,887
single women, 1038 widows, and 745 married,
or 4 % of the whole. But widows were 6 % of the
whole, so that those who had passed under the
protection of a mate were, taken together, 10 % of
all these working women,—fairly representative
of the whole. These numbers do not include
either factory operatives or professional women.

Diffused through the entire community, and
varied by the marriage relations and episodic
"support" of shorter or longer duration, these
women and their work are apt to make as little
impression on the imagination of the community
as did the large artisan vote in England, before
it was discovered in 1866.

" These artisans, forming 26 % of the borough constitu-
ents, kept the secret so well, their votes were so devoid
of any traceable consequence, they had all this power of
shaking our institutions and so obstinately persisted in
not doing it, that now these gentlemen are quite alarmed,
and recoil in terror from the abyss into which they have
not fallen. . . 26 % concentrated would be a considerable representation ; but 26 % diffused may be almost the
same as none at all." *

This is true for the average imagination, but
is no longer permissible when we are considering the philosophy of it, which is bound to
account for everything. Rude empiricism may,
but philosophy may not, stigmatize as " abnormal " 360,000 or 3,000,000 women ; simply
because wrens, sparrows, and polygamic hens
seem always to get provided with mates. Apart
from its inaccuracy, it is rather cruel to affix
this stigma of "abnormality" upon unmarried
women, even those who remain unmarried all
their lives, who are fortunately very much in
the minority. It is surely enough to be obliged,
in a crooked world, to remain denied the possession of husband and children, but these
women must also suffer the depressing influence
of a stigma, of being counted organically
wrong in the scheme of things. Is it not

* John Stuart Mill, *Hansard*, vol. 182, col. 1256.

enough that one set of faculties are denied expansion, but all must be compressed and shriv-
elled through inaction? On the other hand,
apart from cruelty and inaccuracy, this theory
of the "abnormal" is highly unphilosophical,
since the test of the norm is not derived from
human society, but from something else. Since
this society, under almost all known circumstances, always does contain a varying minority
of unmated adults of both sexes, why is it not
fair to conclude that this circumstance, though
exceptional in a lesser social organism, is really
essential to the larger one of human beings?

What is the proof of organic fitness, except
constancy of organ, and proved and permanent
utility of function? Both conditions obtain
for celibates in human society, and for celibate
women far more than for celibate men.

If we turn from abstractions, and appeal to
the senses, which are "at short range so despotic," let the thoughtful observer enter the
city cars at any time between seven and nine
every morning, and study the throng of women,
young and old, who also are going out to their
labor until evening—the clerks, typewriters,
stenographers, saleswomen, book-keepers, cash-
iers, later the teachers; or let him stand at a busy

corner on Broadway at six in the evening, and watch the crowds pouring out from the retail stores,* the binderies, printing establishments, newspaper offices; or let him, either morning or evening, try to visit the ring of ferries encircling the city, and analyze into their component sexes the vast crowds pouring in and out from the suburbs; or, at some railway station at a factory town, watch the operatives disembarking from the train for their day's work;—after a single day of such inspection, the observer, if thoughtful and attentive, would find it hard to get away from the vivid impression, hard to believe that any women remained at home to sew and dust and sweep or mind the babies. And, to his imagination, the "women of leisure" would disappear as completely as, in the United States, the men of leisure are wiped out of the national census.

If the refusal of the sovereignty to women were really due to the fact that they did no work and had male protectors to work for them, like queen bees, then whenever they did work, or had no male protectors, the right of franchise should logically have been accorded. This has

---

* There are 1400 women employed in one Sixth Avenue store alone, in all its departments.

never been done. The grant of municipal franchise to spinsters and widows in England is
not made to them, but to the property they
may happen to hold, since it is only when they
have property that they are supposed to need
protection, and the absence of a male protector
to be inconvenient. No women could have
worked harder, and more obviously on a level
with their men, in respect of endurance, courage,
and heroism, and even intelligence, than the
wives of the colonists who founded this country. Yet no one dreamed of according a share
in the crown to those who so valiantly held up
their end of the cross. The act of shooting
Indians from a stockade seemed to our fore-
fathers, as to our contemporaries, so meritorious,
that it deserved all the sovereignty it could
get. The acts of nursing families through the
small-pox, of bearing famine, or grinding the
scanty corn, seemed too trifling for social recognition.

The contrasting circumstances of the women
who, for the moment, live at ease in New York
to-day, bring no contrast in their political status.
Where sovereignty is, as has for centuries generally been the case, associated with wealth,
rank, and leisure, women are excluded because

they were considered fit only for drudgery.
When, through the widening of the franchise,
the balance of power tends to shift to those who
work, the women are again excluded, on the
ground that they do not work hard enough!
Cœlum non animum mutant!

Then is forgotten for women what is so emphatically remembered in regard to men—that
the development of civilization in increasing activities increases the number of activities which
are occupied with other objects than getting a living. As a man's fortune increases, his wife, who
at first perhaps did all her own housework, is
enabled to hire servants, and busy herself with
"social duties." Substitute the words "public,"
"political," for "social" affairs, and a situation
is defined wherein an educated, energetic, intelligent leisure class is encouraged to devote its
energies to the discussion of innumerable problems, quite remote from its own support, which
is secured, or from its own defence—which is not
endangered. The leisure class, which arises in
every community so soon as enough wealth has
accumulated to support it, is the equivalent on
the large social scale for the woman of leisure,
whose energies, released from drudgery, are
liberated for finer, yet not less strenuous and

useful activities by the wealth of her individual family.

Notwithstanding the "support" afforded, and which has seemed to men so liberal, a standing complaint of women, since they have acquired articulate utterance, has always been their poverty; complaint for some purposes, preferred more emphatically by married women than by those who earn their own living. In all countries but America, undowered women have experienced much difficulty in finding mates, who, in marrying a dowry, were certainly relieved — as in the case of Petruchio—of much of the burden of "support." Then the inheritance, even in America, has passed with little reserve into the hands of the husband, who certainly was thereby relieved of much of the necessity of combining with other "mates" for the "provision" of their respective families. Then, when women had no inheritance, they were (and are) supposed to marry for a livelihood, and the bare livelihood being accorded, they were not expected to ask for anything else. Attempts at combination among women for any purpose have been constantly blocked by their inability to put their hands in their pockets to meet any expenses, inasmuch as social activities

were not counted among the necessities of existence comprised under the term "livelihood."

The withdrawal of household industries into
larger spheres, the consequent liberation of the
practical energies of thousands of women, which
until very recently would have thus been entirely absorbed, the awakened consciousness of
the inconvenience of pecuniary dependence, the
re-arrangements of the entire field of labor constantly going on, has already greatly quickened
the industrial capacity of girls, unmarried
women, and widows. The movement is destined
to affect the condition of married women also;
it has already begun to do so, it will do so increasingly in the future, as work is increasingly
recognized to be the normal, and not the abnormal, condition of human beings.

We think the foregoing considerations should
considerably qualify the presumed impertinence
of women's "interference" with the public
affairs, which have, as Dr. Curtis succinctly
shows, developed out of primitive combinations
for "provision." Certainly at no time could
women be less vitally interested in these than
men, especially on Dr. Curtis' showing, for who
can be more concerned about provision than
those who are to be fed? "Inexperience" is

alleged as a reason for rejecting the counsels of women in such matters. Sometimes there is something in this excuse, since it is naturally difficult for any class of people to become experienced in matters which they are forcibly prevented from having anything to do with. At other times, however, the special experience of even the "nesting" woman may be of value in the councils of valiant man. For instance, if the primitive community were discussing an improvement in stone arrow-heads, it is possible that the female members could add little to the discussion—at least, on the unlikely assumption that they were not in the habit of ever taking a hand in shooting for themselves. But if the discussion happened to turn on the time of the year most favorable for hunting, these same women, if permitted to speak, might have suggested, from their own observation, that at certain seasons slaughter of the does would risk extermination of the game. So, many ages later, when English manufacturers were torturing women and young children to death in factories, their own husbands and fathers aiding, it is conceivable, had the natural instincts and faculties of the millowners' wives had free play, they might have suggested that under this system the race could be exterminated or fatally degenerated. But the English lady—trained, if not bound, to her "nest"—was as mute as her prehistoric ancestress, who watched by the camp-fire while the braves chattered at a distance.

•

VI.

PLAUSIBLE as is the theory which limits "interference" in public affairs to those who may claim some experience in them, no one who attentively considers the conduct of even modern States will venture to assert that this theory is realized in practice. Indeed, it never has been so realized. The suggestion that people should undertake to learn something about things before they undertook to dogmatize or to act in reference to them is a daring innovation on all established precedent. It is not only in Tammany-ridden New York that expert knowledge seems at a discount,—they *don't* do these things any better in France, nor in England. Herbert Spencer ridicules the House of Commons for paying more attention to the knowledge its members may have of Horace, than of sanitary engineering, even those to whom may be entrusted the work requiring engineering experts.

"And if an institution undertakes not two functions, but a score,—if a government, whose office it is to defend citizens against aggressors, foreign and domestic ; engages also to disseminate Christianity, to administer charity, to teach children their lessons, to adjust prices of food, to inspect coal-mines, to arrange cab-fares, to look into people's stink-traps, to vaccinate their children, to send out emigrants, to prescribe hours of labor, to examine lodging-houses, to test the knowledge of mercantile captains, to provide public libraries, to read and authorize dramas, to inspect passenger-ships, to see that small dwellings are supplied with water, to regulate endless things, from a banker's issues down to the boat-fares on the Serpentine,—it is not manifest that its primary duty must be ill discharged in proportion to the multiplicity of affairs it busies itself with ?" *

Women are not necessarily so "inexperienced" that their advice would always be an intrusion.

From the moment it has been accepted as important that the entire body of the State should be actively alive, alert, and capable ; and that the education of a few dozen experts would not meet the exigencies of the case; from the

* Herbert Spencer, *Essay on Over-Legislation*, 1871, p. 94. This satirical enumeration is guided by Mr. Spencer's favorite dogma of opposition to all State interference. For our purpose the list is more interesting as indicating how various are the functions assumed by the modern State,—how impossible to reason concerning them exclusively from the model of the primitive tribe.

moment that public work became so multifarious
that the community does not by any means yet
furnish a sum total of intelligence adequate to its
requirements,—from that moment it became evident that in every direction much work must be
undertaken which would be badly done. It
would be absurd, however, to pretend that it
was less well done now than formerly. Knowledge and expertise have not been banished from
the world by democracy, but may be said to
have obtained, for the first time, a place of public
power, proportioned to the vastness of public
needs. The filthy cholera pilgrims at Mecca
have become the occasion of researches involving intellectual processes as subtle and refined
as went to the construction of Plato's *Dia-
logues.*

To such new expertise women also can be
trained. They are by no means necessarily so
"inexperienced," that their advice would be an
"intrusion" on the counsels of the State.) Mr.
Spencer shows this incidentally in reference to
the Family Colonization Loan Society, which
Mrs. Chisholm conducted side by side with the
Emigration Board. "Under the government
management hundreds of emigrants die of fever
from close packing, and with its licence vessels

sail which are the homes of fraud, brutality, tyranny, and obscenity. Under the woman's, better accommodation than ever before is provided; it does not demoralize by promiscuous crowding, but improve by mild discipline; it does not pauperize by charity, but encourages providence; it does not increase our taxes, but is self-supporting. The State is beaten by a woman ! " *

So great is the present differentiation of the functions of " provision " and " defence," that we do not expect the same group of people to concern themselves about both. Merchants attend to one, soldiers to the other. The last improbability of war is supposed to have been reached when a people has been characterized as a " nation of shopkeepers."

How, then, can the personal incapacity of women for " defence " constitute sufficient ground to exclude them from all interest, voice, and power in public affairs? Is the Chamber of Commerce identical with the Brooklyn Navy Yard? Is the Produce Exchange manned by officers from West Point? This question of "defence"—so constantly occurring in this discussion—is scarcely ever adjusted to the

* *Loc. cit.*, p. 79.

8

methods of making or declaring war which are actually adopted in the United States of America. A New England town meeting does not declare war like the Athenian Ecclesia. Even in the Roman Republic, decisions of peace and war were not left to popular assemblies or popular vote; not even to the will of consuls or commanders of armies. The fateful choice rested exclusively with the Senate. With us, every one knows, who stops to think, that the proclamation of war, the ratification of peace, are functions reserved for the Senate and President of the United States, and removed from the control of even the State governments. At what point, therefore, except through the formation of public opinion, could the popular vote of women influence any decision for war? The presence of a few women in the United States Senate is, indeed, a theoretic possibility, but so very remote it need scarcely enter into the present discussion.

By the "intrusion of inexperienced women into the councils of the State," is probably meant, however, the exertion of such influence as may be brought to bear upon legislature through elections, and upon administration, through a share in administrative appoint-

ments. Legislation and civil administration
which do not directly decide any question of
war, and but few questions of industry, do undoubtedly exercise much indirect influence on
both. The public opinion behind them in a
free state does, if possible, still more, and one of
the most immediate and direct results of woman
suffrage would be a great increase in the contribution of woman to the formation of public
opinion.

Granted; but in what way can it then be
shown, that the questions so submitted to legislatures, administrations, or public opinion—
whether of peace or war; whether of industry,
commerce, social regulations or public morals;
whether material or spiritual—do not concern
women, do not naturally interest women, do not
fall within the competence of women exactly to
the extent to which they concern, interest, or
may be discussed by corresponding bodies of
men ?

VII.

TAKE any series of measures as concrete examples : the Missouri Compromise, the election of Lincoln, the election of Maynard, the New York Speedway Bill.

Not one of these measures could be said to stand in any tangible relation with the function of men to provide for either the support or the defence of their respective families. The Missouri Compromise was not brought to popular vote, but decided by Congress, under the more or less remote influence of public opinion, as expressed by the elections of Congressmen, and through the public press while congressional debate was going on. Through no other agencies could the popular opinion in the matter make itself felt. Does Dr. Curtis mean, that a well bred American husband should say to his wife, "You have no right to have any opinion on this matter, because I pay our rent, gas, and coal bills "? He would have the right, and the laws of the State of New York would support him in insisting upon it, to say that, as he is responsible for the house rent, his wife must agree to live where his judgment decides is the best place to make money. But what law, or (present) custom, admits that the same circumstance gives him a right to control his wife's opinion ? But if this may not be controlled, why may it not be expressed, and expressed effectively, in the only way in which it can be effective,—through the ballot ? *The gravest consequence of denying the right to an effective opinion is, that this denial soon atrophies the power to form a just opinion.* The greatest importance of democracy, the attribute that brings it into line with the most abstract theory of general evolution, is its power to develop power in the masses upon whom it has been conferred. To the democratic constitution of Kleisthenes the Athenians owed at once their triumph in the Persian wars, and the intellectual splendor of their age of Pericles.

The popular will was much more distinctly and directly expressed in the election of Lincoln, and, as every one knew at the time, this momentous occasion not only decided the choice of an individual, but practically accepted the challenge to civil war. This is the only moment in American history, from the settlement of Jamestown or the landing of the Pilgrims, where a popular election has involved such a decision, or met any such severe and sharply defined crisis. It would have been therefore a much more practical test of the propriety of a woman vote on questions involving war, than most of the elections which occurred during the Missouri Compromise controversy.

In this momentous decision, can it be suggested that women were not equally concerned and interested with men ? Can it even be maintained that there were not thousands as well informed on the questions at issue as the men who cast their ballots on that November day, 1860? Did the women who followed their husbands to Kansas, in that mighty Free Soil emigration, know nothing about it ? Did the women who for thirty years had sustained a full half of the abolition agitation, know nothing about it? And what should have prevented every woman from knowing about it in November, as every one through the length and breadth of the land did in April,—except the laws and

customs which, by forcibly excluding them
from participation in political affairs, as forcibly condemned them to apathy on great and
public questions?

The election of Maynard in 1893 might, from
one point of view, be considered to turn upon
questions too technical for any but lawyers to
understand. It was, however, thrown upon
public notice in such a way that it became
a question of public morals. Have women no
interest in public morals? Because their husbands may remain, in New England phrase,
"good providers," under various situations of
public demoralization, from that of the Tweed
Ring to that of the Second Empire, need women
take no thought of the moral standard of the
community? Are those Kentucky women to
blame who have been exerting themselves to
defeat Breckinridge? Are they "meddling"
with what does not belong to them?

And finally, minute in its scope as compared
with the mighty piece of legislation which
headed our list, the Speedway Bill is yet especially interesting as an example of municipal
concern. Did women have no interest in that?
If the Park was not for women and children
for whom was it intended? Why then should

they not have been permitted to join, even more directly than they did, in the successful effort to resist the shameless, though petty depredation?

A remark stands ready at hand, in reply to all that has just been said. All these measures were carried out by men, without the aid of women. What advantage then would it have been for them to have lent or rather intruded their aid? The Missouri Compromise was made; the Missouri Compromise was repealed; Lincoln was elected and re-elected; the little Speed-way ferment formed and subsided. The women were never "in it"; but what was the harm? If women were unintelligent or indifferent in these matters, the less they had to do with them the better. If they were intelligent enough to sit at home and think them all out for themselves, they could only applaud the success of the exertions of their "mates" and "providers." *" Qui fecit per alium, fecit per se."*

The trouble is that, under such adjustment, the women, precisely like men in similar circumstances, who have no chance to do, acquire no power to think, and the power to think is the ultimate though unconscious aim of all democratic activities. In a democratic republic, the Public Life is the visible expression of the Man thinking, to whom each individual man must incessantly return. "Cut off from that, the farmer becomes the plough, the sailor the rope, the thinker the bookworm " *; the woman, we might add, the sex. This is the meaning of our American State. It is not merely a congeries of households, whose male representatives cross their thresholds in the morning to find something to eat for their families, and pay taxes to maintain the police. It is a vast, real, living organism, with most complex functions, most subtle yet mighty vital processes, most glorious of vital powers.

"Methinks I see in my mind a noble and puissant nation rousing herself like a strong man after sleep, and stroking her invincible locks : methinks I see her as an eagle mewing her mighty youth, and kindling her un-dazzled eyes at the full midday beam ; . . . while the whole noise of timorous and flocking birds, with those also that love the twilight, flutter about amazed at what she means." †

This organism cannot be constructed like a brick wall, in segments of caste or class, adjacent, superposed according to long traditions of place or etiquette of precedence. Its elements must be individual cells, grouping themselves into

---

* Emerson, *American Scholar*.   † Areopagitica.

organs according to their individual affinities
and capacities—the microscopic function of
each, ennobled by its relationship to the whole;
the healthful activity of the whole, insured by
the punctual action of these parts.

Confessedly, in embracing in this conception
women, we do introduce a change; a change
which, though in itself purely ideal, underlies
all the practical issues now in dispute. In this
essentially modern conception, women also are
brought into direct relations with the State, independent of their "mates" or their "brood."
Yet is this audacious proceeding justified by
one simple fact—women already stand in this
relation.

It is probably on this account that Mr. Goldwin Smith declares that woman suffrage aims
at such a "sexual revolution" as must cause
the "dissolution of the family." The suffrage
claim does not aim at this: it seeks only to
formulate, recognize, and define the revolution
already effected, yet which leaves the family
intact. The *Patria Potestas* is gone; a man has
lost, first, the right to kill his own son; then
the right to order the marriage of his daughter;
then the right to absorb the property of his
wife. Nevertheless, he survives, and the family,

shorn of its portentous rights, bids fair in America to remain the happiest of all conceivable natural institutions; more profound than society, so immeasurably deeper than politics, that the fortunate wife, daughter, or sister is puzzled when the two are mentioned in the same breath.

A natural institution reposes on the facts of nature, and is limited by them. When the natural right of women to maintenance is based on maternity, not only firmly, but exclusively, many practical consequences will gradually ensue. Women married at thirty, and liable to be left widows between forty and fifty, will not consider their entire lives summed up within fifteen years; will prepare for self-support and other activities both before and after. Still more so the women who never marry. Childless women will recognize that their pecuniary dependence on their husbands rests on an entirely different basis from that of mothers. In many cases they would choose that such dependence should not exist at all. In others the tendency, now alleged to be so widespread, to avoid maternity would be checked; as in the ancient cruel times when a woman could be divorced for childlessness.

Maternity itself will be recognized to be though in one aspect so intensely personal, yet in another, a social function, with the very widest social consequences. Thus it is precisely the relation in which begins that "close association with her mate," which is supposed to exclude the woman from all social association, which, more philosphically understood, cannot fail to bring women into the widest, most fundamental, and most direct relation with the State.

Representative government did not originate in America; but, for modern times, individual representation did. The division into the Three Estates, to which allusion has already been made, as affected in the middle of the thirteenth century, completed the transformation, gradually carried on during preceding centuries, of the basis of representation from individuals, to that of classes, groups, orders, interests, organizations. This conception of representation has become so profoundly imbedded in the English mind, that a franchise reposing on a manhood basis does, almost to this very day, seem to Englishmen too " monotonous," or too "French!"

VIII.

THE Three Estates were never organized in America: the general equality of social conditions forbade. Yet the theory and practice of individual representation, of manhood suffrage, did not arise simply in this historic situation. It is logically traceable to a great new Idea, which is literally at the very central core of the American Union, and without which that Federal Union could never have been founded. The discovery of this "brand new idea," as it was at first called, solved the apparently insoluble difficulty of co-adjusting State governments with a national existence. The discovery is *that the national government should act upon individuals, and not on States.*

"In February, 1783, Pelatiah Webster published at Philadelphia a tract, in which he advocated a national assembly with power, not only to enact the laws, but to enforce them on individuals as well as on States. A year later this tract was followed by another of the same tenor by Noah Webster, in which he proposed 'a new system of government which should act, not on the States, but directly on individuals.'" *

So great was the force of this idea that it not only made the American Union, but it swept the dwelling of the new republic clean of the vast conglomerate of groups and institutions, which in England everywhere intervene between the State and the individual. The complicated balance of franchise rights, which in England still persists in the midst of nearly universal suffrage, and which justifies itself by historic inheritance, could not have existed on this continent, where the idea of the individual had become necessary and fundamental. If State governments were not to interpose between the National Power and the men of the State, certainly no lesser organization of class or caste, or family, or association with savings banks, or universities, or poor-rates, or "ancient rights" could do so. The "compound householder" and the laborious discussions and mathematical calculations to which he

* *Madison Papers*, vol. ii., p. 708, quoted by Hannis Taylor, *loc. cit.*

gave rise, * must always have been as impossible in the United States as a reanimated
megatherium. We believe that much of the
" straightness and lucidity," which Matthew
Arnold attributes to the American mind, is due
exactly to the fact that at the moment of the birth
of the American Nation, a straight path was made
right from the Central Power to the ultimate
units of the State, and no deviations were permitted through interposed organizations, ready
to encrust and complicate with every year of time.
Ennobled by this direct radiation from the Central Power, each unit became a man, and each
man a unit. The need of " making a voter out
of a man " by long and intricate and gradual
process was abolished in advance. Manhood
suffrage in America may seem to result, his-
torically, from the general average equality of
social conditions among the inhabitants of the
thirteen States. But it may also be deduced as
a philosophical necessity from the Idea of Individualism, which became the core of the Federal Union.

This idea, at first suggested only for men,
has, little by little, spread to women also. In
law, the family, the father, the husband, no

* In the English debates on the Reform Bills for 1866-1867.

longer intervenes between the woman and the State; no organization complicates the direct relation. ⅄Women pay their own taxes, both State and Federal: direct, when these are imposed; indirect, whenever they are supporting themselves and buying commodities. ⋅ They appear in the law courts in their own persons, not by the intermediary of husband, guardian, or trustees. They are directly liable for all the engagements they may enter into in their own names, and their contracts will be enforced directly by the State upon them or upon whichever party in their contract may be delinquent. Only when, in incurring household expenses, or personal expenses while at the head of a married family, and when they are therefore presumed to act as the agents of their husbands, are women in New York placed in any different relation with the State from men.

Thus, women are really recognized as individuals, in the same way as men; so that the pressure to obtain all individual rights for those who already have all individual liabilities and responsibilities, is so logical as to become well-nigh irresistible. In a second and more symbolic sense, the modern, American, New York individualism of women has a peculiarly interesting significance. The habit of thought, which has removed men from the grasp of lesser groups and organizations and brought their personalities into immediate relation with the State; and not only with the domiciliary State, but with the whole Federal Union, and this not successively, but simultaneously; so that a man is at the same moment a citizen of New York and an American; this same conception, endorsed by actual fact, justifies the emancipation of women from their exclusive classification within the limits of the family, and declares that while they are members of that, they are, coincidently, members, citizens of the State.

But this view reverses the entire Roman-law view of the status of women. Therefore, according to Goldwin Smith (and some others), it determines the "dissolution of the family." Be it noted, however, that the suffrage—which has not yet been conferred—is not responsible for these pangs of dissolution, and the latter, moreover, do not seem to be the pangs of death !

Though the suffrage be not the cause of this change, it is certainly irresistibly suggested as the immediate sequence. A direct relation with the State as a unit, in a State where such direct

10

relation everywhere, and always, over vast ranges of territory and through enormous masses of population, carries with it political representation and political rights,—how can it fail to do so in this case also? Women have hitherto been deprived of political right and representation, precisely for the reason Dr. Curtis alleges: the State was constituted exclusively by the men outside a certain pale, and dealt with those within almost exclusively through the intermediary of the others. This being no longer the case, and many illusions having been destroyed as to the reality of previously alleged representation and protection, no excuse remains for longer deferring the right of representation accorded to other units of the American Union.

When the theory of individualism has once been realized fully in fact, women would lose that tendency " to work apart from other mated females." which Dr. Curtis, no less than Goethe recognizes.

Dr. Curtis has defined this tendency and its cause with admirable terseness and precision; he has failed, however, to show why it should be considered admirable. Indubitably it lies at the root of the entire anti-suffrage movement

among women, of whom large numbers have
never been accustomed to think of themselves
as "gregarious animals, capable of concerted
action for mutual advantage." To what is female jealousy due, so far as it is a mental habit
and not justified by the occasion, except the deep-
rooted instinct which contemplates all women
exclusively from their possible relation to some
one man? In this way, at present, is often
curtailed the usefulness of much philanthropic
exertion among women, the effectiveness of
many advisory boards. The women on these
boards, like to advise men, who are not thereby
seriously embarrassed, but they make little effort
to establish a situation in which their advice
could be carried out by other women. Like
the anxious housewife, who avoids engaging a
competent housekeeper, lest her comeliness prove
too attractive to the master of the house, they
often prefer to do it all themselves, or to leave
it undone.

Admirable in its conception as was the State
Charities Aid Association, there is a striking
contrast between the efficiency of its initial
work, the reformation of Bellevue Hospital,
and anything, for instance, which has been
effected on the Islands. In the first case the

reform was re-enforced by a fruitful new idea,—
a Training School for Nurses was established,—
the first in the country.   By this a new sphere
of action was opened to women, who rushed
into it; their ambition, self-interest, and enthusiasm were enlisted to carry out the work which
had been planned.   The result was an unquali-
fied success.   Where elsewhere has such a
success been scored ?

That women themselves offer a field, a large
field, a field as large as half the population of
the world for the activities of women, seems to
be one of the youngest ideas of recorded time.
That women can be the pupils, patients, clients,
and customers of women, as well as their servants and patronized objects of charity, is just
beginning to be suspected.   Following along
this line of thought, it is easy to foresee women
as captains in industry as well as beneficiaries,
interesting themselves to ameliorate the lot of
women industrials, who have become something
else to them than only the employees of their
own husbands or fathers.   It is easy to foresee
women, in their political relations with the
State, undertaking to guide and influence the
action of other women, who also hold political
relations with the State, but whose relative,

personal or social dependence persists. They may begin in their own kitchens; they may end by creating political forces which shall often serve to counterpoise the votes of ignorant or interested men.

"Equal rights for all is only equal rights in the same thing for all the similarly conditioned as to the same thing." True, and the "same thing" is vital representation in a social organism where all elements, whose wants, ideas, and will are not represented, are only socially half alive. The "similarly conditioned" are, in our existing situation, any adult male who is of sane mind and not an actual inmate of a penal institution. Among these are thousands, most "inexperienced" in regard to the questions they help more or less to decide; thousands who are "irresponsible, since under no circumstances would they be required to enforce the measures that might be decided upon by their advice;" and "different," if not "organically," yet so markedly, in nationality, inheritance, education, training, intelligence, circumstance, and point of view, that the mental differences between the American man and his wife shrink to nothing in comparison.

And whatever peevish carpers may assert, it

is not true that the equal political representation of this vast mass of the inexperienced, the
irresponsible, and the different has worked
badly; has not indeed worked better than any
other system hitherto devised. The system
simply removes previous shackles, opens un-
bounded opportunity to all forces to contend
together in the public arena until the strongest
prevail. Vice gets no more chance than under
any other system. But if poverty, ignorance,
and vulgarity have more "show," nothing is
done to detract from the natural force of wealth,
knowledge, and refinement. If the force of
these decline, if their rightful superiority abate,
it is from internal decay, not from external
pressure; and the remedy must be found in
forces deeper than political system. Our
scholars in politics do not at present write
the Areopagitica; but the times are perchance
not strenuous enough to engender such high
thought.

In this interregnum of lax and facile time,
the one new, great, powerful thought that has
moved swiftly to the front, is that of the
enfranchisement of women.

Let the thought achieve its own realization.

IX.

A FTER all, it is not a theory but a situation which confronts us. What is it?

In New York State, according to the census of 1890, there is a total population of 5,997,853, of which 3,020,960 are female; 2,976,893 are male. The proportion of women to men in the State is, therefore, as $1\frac{1}{67}$ to 1, or sensibly equal. The slight excess (44,067) of female population in the State is counterbalanced for the whole United States by an excess of males. For the whole country there are 32,067,880 males and 30,554,370 females; an excess of males of 1,513,510. This excess is mainly due to immigration; since, for many past decades, the female immigrants from Europe have been annually less than the number of males. At the last count, June 30, 1893, there had been during the preceding year only four females to eleven males among the immigrants."* In the

---

* *Statistics Bearing on Equal Suffrage*, Adèle M. Fielde. Suffrage Leaflets, 11th Assembly District Committee.

State of New York, which alone concerns us, the men of voting age numbered 1,769,649. As the total female population was sensibly equal to the male, being only $\frac{1}{68}$ in excess; it may be assumed that there are an equal number of women of voting age.

This number of the total female population, in round numbers, three million, corresponds pretty closely with the number of women in the entire country engaged in "gainful occupations." The imperfect census of 1890 gives no tables of occupations. But the census of 1880 gives the number of women in all classes of occupations as 2,647,157, a number which has certainly increased to over three million in the last fourteen years. In 1779, in the middle year of the Revolutionary War, the white population of the United States was about 2,175,000.* This number, two and one half million, seems to mark the point at which an impulse for independence becomes urgent if not irresistible.

The proposal to enfranchise (in round numbers) 1,500,000 persons in a total adult population of three million, invites the inquiry:

1st. What precedents exist for such a measure of enfranchisement ?

---

* Fiske, *Critical Period of American History*, p. 102.

2d. To what extent would the new voters be homogeneous with the old, or to what extent would their heterogeneity constitute a disturbing element?

3d. What special circumstances of religion, nationality, social condition, or civil status would require consideration in respect to such newly enfranchised persons?

4th. What circumstances connected with their previously unenfranchised condition could be presumed to be influential after enfranchisement?

5th. Whether, apart from the general advantage of public representation—now firmly recognized as a general principle in every modern State,—any special advantages would be likely to arise from the enfranchisement of the particular class now claiming the suffrage.

In discussions on Woman Suffrage, the precedents alleged are usually those of Wyoming and Colorado, where full suffrage for women now exists; New Zealand, where full parliamentary suffrage has just been granted to women; municipal suffrage, as it exists in England, Canada, and Kansas; or school suffrage, as it exists in twenty-three States of the American Union.

The important facts about the suffrage in Wyoming, Colorado, and New Zealand are: 1st. That the suffrage is there complete, and not partial. It does not differentiate women from other voters, and in the American States presupposes no property or other special qualifications, such as are associated with school suffrage. 2d. Under these circumstances, during the twenty-five years the franchise has been exercised in Wyoming, and at the single elections held under it in Colorado and New Zealand,—the woman vote has been called out very fully. In the recently enfranchised States, the enthusiasm, at least on this one occasion, has been immense. 3d. The extremely sparse population of Wyoming, which could not fairly be said to justify its admission as a State, is said to throw its case out of comparison with a much more thickly populated State, as New York. Yet for the philosophers who are always endeavoring to study the woman question in outline, in type, in primitive beginnings, the relative simplicity of this situation should render it as valuable as village communities and town meetings have been found by the student of political evolution.

4th. In one respect, contradictory reports have reached us from Wyoming, or more specifically from Cheyenne. It has been asserted that in cities still bearing the imprint of mining towns, the proportion of women of the courtesan class was relatively large, and that their vote had been handled by interested election agents,—in the same way as the Italian vote in New York is handled by the padrone. If this be true, this section of the Wyoming vote must be simply compared with the Italian and other controlled vote in New York;—a form of rude and primitive suffrage, that constitutes a sort of survival of antique forms in the midst of civilization, and cannot but be destined to disappear. It is simply impossible to compare this vote with the vote of women of any other class,—and even if it were true that all such women voted, their total number in the city of New York is not registered as more than 40,000, out of a total population of between 1,500,000 and 2,000,000.

In another place, the argument from this special possibility—which so strangely jostles upon sentimental arguments of such a precisely opposite character,—has been considered from another point of view. At this place we can note, notwithstanding the hysteric excitement which has been displayed in some quarters in regard to this topic, that other information declares the alleged reports are not true. The wholesome law which compels every one to register at a certain time before voting, acts as a deterrent upon those, and especially upon women, who do not wish their names or calling to be forced into publicity. This fact is itself sufficient to meet the immediate apprehension. The changes in the entire situation which the future may bring about are too remote, and the considerations involved too delicate and complex for present discussion.

Certainly, however, if any attitude of mind can be considered fantastic, it is that by which a professedly sober man can call himself "outraged" at the thought that a woman of his family should deposit a vote at the polls the moment before or after a woman of this "class" might by chance have done the same. This form of social "contamination" is certainly most attenuated.

5th. The situation in Colorado was specialized by the insertion of woman-suffrage "planks" in the platforms of the county conventions, by the Republicans and also the Populist party. In New York State no such party endorsement of woman suffrage has ever been obtained, and on that account Miss Anthony seems to think that

New York cannot be carried in its favor. However, in 1892, the New York State Legislature, at that time with a Democratic majority, not only brought to its third reading a bill in favor of woman suffrage, but carried it through the Assembly. Under the circumstances such a vote could only be looked upon as a declaration of opinion; but as such it was certainly significant.

6th. One other fact from Colorado is very interesting. As soon as the constitutional amendment had been carried, and the first election held, women, having "received their baptism of fire," began, all over the country, to organize clubs for the serious study of political institutions. Is it on record that any other class of newly enfranchised voters ever did the same?

In New Zealand, the remarkable fact of the election was that the women, having been enfranchised by one party, voted chiefly for the candidate of the other.

This same independence was also shown at the first municipal elections held in Kansas. To the women's vote was largely due the defeat of the Populists and the Republican victory, although the Populists had been mainly instrumental in the enfranchisement of women. Several noted but undesirable "leaders," among others Mrs. Lease, were "snowed under" by the vote of the women.

Nothing could be of better augury for the future of woman suffrage than indications of its independence of political parties. Whatever be the function of parties in a system of representative government, it is evident that much of their machinery is excessively clumsy; much of their action requires to be supplemented by other than strict party motives. The assumption that any one party is always right, even on issues other than that in which it originated, is theoretically absurd. Party allegiance must usually, in modern times, with their nicely complex issues, be a matter of expediency, and may be usefully traversed by many other expediencies, such as voters less trained to party discipline would be most likely to suggest.

Municipal suffrage in England and Canada constitutes very little precedent for our proposed situation.

" In the northern countries of the Germanic world, the communal right . . . accepts, as the qualification, possession of real property, without regard to the person. . . . Property has become the exclusive basis of the right, the personality of the owner is completely disregarded, the difference between the sexes is thenceforth an idle distinction. Among Germans, Anglo-Saxons, Scandinavians, where communal right has a real as opposed to a personal basis, woman is admitted to the enjoyment of it. . . . Therefore, while granting the communal right to women (as well as to companies and corporations), by virtue of their property right, care has been taken to limit it to that sphere of local self-government which is devoid of all political character, and concerned chiefly with the administration of the economic interests of the place. . . .

" In 1888, women rate-payers were included among the electors to the county councils, but were not considered eligible for election." *

This obstinate restriction of franchise right to property, ingeniously enucleates the cardinal, vital value of the suffrage. Such franchise does not enhance—it depresses the dignity of the human unit who exercises it, not in virtue of himself, but of the non-human thing to which he is appended. The value in the development of the effective force of persons of these local, communal, municipal rights of suffrage seems to increase the nearer we mount to their origin. When land ownership meant freedom, and the landless were dependent cultivators, laets,† and slaves, the vote of the freeman was a sign of

---

* Ostrogorski, *loc. cit.* pp. 90 and 101.

† Kemble, *Saxons in England*, quoted by Hannis Taylor, *loc. cit.* p. 126.

personal dignity, as well as property.   Now that
there are freemen who do not own land—freemen who have more political rights than some
of the persons (the women) who do own land,
—the vote accorded to such possession has been
emptied of half its value. The refusal to extend
Parliamentary suffrage to women who are possessed of municipal suffrage, does not mean, as
Americans are apt to suppose, that women are
counted able to judge about the small concerns
of a town, but not about Imperial issues.   It
means that women are still not counted able to
exercise an independent judgment at all, and,
therefore, are to remain counted out when this
is called for ; but that the property to which they
happen to belong, and which requires representation, must not be deprived of this on account
of an entangling female alliance.

This is the very antipodes of the Democratic
doctrine, perhaps also somewhat excessive, that
a *man* requires representation so much that he
must not be deprived of it on account of the
accident of being unable to read and write.

Absurd doctrine, from some points of view.
Yet what other has ever been able to secure for
every one the opportunity to learn how to read
and write ?

For the above reasons, it is plain that the proposal often broached, indeed submitted, to many of our State Legislatures to confer municipal suffrage upon women as a partial and tentative measure, is based on a misapprehension of English precedent. Municipal suffrage in Kansas demands no property qualification, and its exercise therefore does not differ in the least from that required in a Presidential election. On the other hand, as the municipal concerns of New York and other large cities offer at present the most complex and perplexing problems with which the present time has to grapple, municipal suffrage is not the simplest task to be learned first, but precisely the most difficult and most arduous. The "vote that comes down to the Harlem River" now often serves to correct the local aberrations of the New York vote. Such correction would be needed as much for the vote of women as of men.

School suffrage is a form of partial suffrage which might, much more rationally than municipal suffrage, be used as a preliminary tentative form of enfranchisement, where a preliminary experiment were deemed essential. It necessitates very properly either some educa-

11

tional and some property qualification, or some special relation to the children going to school. The pertinence of the influence of women in school matters is to-day so generally admitted, the mental change since 1821 is so enormous, that men generally say : "Yes, women should vote for school officers, and be elected to School Boards "; and women continually sign petitions for this privilege, till startled by the discovery that it also means something else. It means, however, in the State of New York, according to the decision of its Supreme Court, that women can only enjoy this privilege thoroughly if empowered by constitutional amendment to vote for all officers as well as for School Commissioner.

Further, in the great cities of New York and Brooklyn, where the Mayor appoints the Boards of Education, and the School Trustees are appointed by them, the only way in which women can effectively reach the schools is by sharing in the election for Mayor.

Twenty-three States other than New York have conferred school suffrage upon women. The right is so new, the mental habits of women and capacity for collective action have been as yet so little tested, that little can be learned about the effect of women's voting from the history of school suffrage. Complaints of apathy, of special parsimony on the part of women taxpayers, of lack of initiative in the improvement of education, are easily made. Sometimes such complaints are well founded and incidental to a transition state of things. Quite as often they are radically unjust, and overlook tangible instances of valuable aid rendered by women to the schools, to schooling, or to the action of officials.

Because women should be, from their natural relations and from the extent to which the business of teaching has fallen into their hands, peculiarly interested in school government and administration, it does not follow that under hitherto existing conditions they have had opportunities to receive the requisite training even for theoretic thought. When it comes to practical action they are blocked at every step by the circumstances of their political restrictions. How can women attempt to remedy the often disgraceful material conditions of New York schools, * when they have nothing to do with taxation (except to pay their own taxes), and

* The *Evening Post*, April 2, 1894, article headed "Condition of the Schools ; Shocking Effects of what the Mayor Calls Economy."

not the slightest influence with the Boards of Estimate and Apportionment? How may women increase the efficiency of teachers, dispirited by unequal salaries and cowed by machine rule, when they confront the immovable determination in all public administrations to accord for the same grade of work higher salaries to voters than to non-voters?

How can women serve, even through the courtesy of appointment, on New York School Boards, when, having gained a footing, they are promptly swept away again by the decision of a new Mayor, who has his own views on the "place for women"? What is wisdom in conservative London may, without appeal, be pronounced nonsense in New York.

The real precedent for the enfranchisement of New York women is hardly ever recognized to be such—we mean the extensions of the franchise effected in England by the Reform Bills of 1832, 1867, and 1884.

A certain class of people enslaved to appear-

"The moral law rules the world: but at short range the senses are despotic."

ances, always cowering before the huge wave of advancing democracy, like children before the

surf on the seashore,—are apt to say : " Democracy, once let loose, proceeds inevitably from
bad to worse to a final culmination (?) of imbecile unfitness. All weak, ignorant, and incom-
petent men have already been added to the
electorate, at least in France, Germany, and
America. It is proposed now to take the lowest
step of all and admit women."

Here is another central grappling knot of the
discussion : We deny, utterly and in toto, that
the extension of suffrage to women implies a
general step downwards in competency. In the
language of the English debates of 1867, what
is demanded is *not* a further vertical extension,
but simply a lateral extension along the lines of
all existing classes. So long as it was assumed
in theory, and often true in fact, that every
woman was necessarily the inferior of every
man in her family—father, brother, husband,
son—in intelligence, education, judgment,
strength of character, woman suffrage might
seem indeed to constitute a vertical extension
downwards, a distinct lowering of the franchise
in dignity and efficiency. Exclusion from the
franchise has been marvellously effective in
perpetuating the reasons which might seem to
justify such exclusion. But this is not more

true of women than of every class permanently
excluded from share in the Sovereignty. Compare the desperately degraded populace of
England at the beginning of the eighteenth
century with the English freemen of the tenth
and eleventh centuries, or even with the upper
class of "landless" men, who came so near the
franchise that the acquisition of a few acres
sufficed to acquire the suffrage.

"I have shown that from the earliest recorded annals,
through nearly three centuries, the condition of the
English laborer was that of plenty and hope,—that from
perfectly intelligible causes it sunk within a century to
so low a level as to make the workmen practically helpless. . . . The first half of the eighteenth century
was still far below the level of the fifteenth." *

The class relations of women have compensated to a certain extent the disabilities of their
sex condition.

This is why Dr. Curtis writes eloquently :

"It must be proved that, in spite of generous law-
making for women, there still lurks in the heart of the
average citizen an innate savage longing to harass and
oppress the mother that gave him being, the wife whom
he invites to share his home, and the daughter whose
sweet devotion is the very sunshine of his life ! "

* Thorold Rogers, *Six Centuries of Work and Wages*, 1884, p. 522.

Even in a time most remote from our own epoch of softened manners, it may be presumed that the legislation and customs which *did* oppress and harass women, did not originate in any "innate savage longing" on the part of men to do so. It was shaped by no harsher sentiment than contempt; and remained for so many years unmodified, for no more definite reasons than forgetfulness of the wrongs of an unobtrusive people, or illusions, which made many of these wrongs seem rights.

"So great a favorite of the English law is the female sex!"

"Admitting," observes Mr. Pellew, "that for some reason or other the Legislature has performed many 'good works for women,' it does not follow that the present system of indirect representation has been a success. Can it be said that it was not until 1874 (in Massachusetts), that it was right to prohibit a husband who had deserted his wife from imposing any restraint on her personal liberty?"

Admitting freely, that in every social class women have shared abundantly in the material advantages and the social position which have been won by the struggles of their "mates," it remains true that until the present century women have been left in a condition of mental degradation, which, for mental purposes, may be very accurately compared with the material degradation of the disfranchised English laborer. We do not speak of exceptions, but of the vast mass of women as compared with the vast mass of men of their own class and families.

" Women may be inferior beings," writes Sydney Smith, "but there really seems to be no reason why a woman of forty should always be as ignorant as a boy of twelve."

" Of women no less than of men it is true that political dependence fosters ignorance and cowardice, and that independence of thought and inquiry is fostered by political independence. It is a legitimate deduction from the history of slaves, of serfs, and of all dependent people, to conclude that it is the absence of the suffrage that keeps so many women, to such a degree, 'ill-educated, bullied, cowardly, bigoted, and empty-headed.' " *

The claim for Woman Suffrage simply emphasizes, endorses, and ratifies the movement of extension of actual value, along lateral class lines, which industrial, legal, and educational movements have already thoroughly begun. It denies that women to-day constitute a universally " weak and dependent class "; just as it was

* George Pellew, *loc. cit.*, p. 36.

denied in 1867 that English artisans, though living in houses of only seven pounds' rental value, must necessarily be drunkards and ready to sell their votes.

"Every man will admit that since the Reform Bill (of 1832) great progress in knowledge and capacity has been make by the working-classes. . . . Can you say that there are not persons below the class of ten-pounds thoroughly fitted for the suffrage, perfectly capable of judgment?" *

Nothing could more vividly illustrate the power of the idea, at once so stubborn and so primitive, which supposes that personalities may be adequately measured and defined by classes, than the debates on the English Reform Bills. It was actually necessary to point out that any of the tests proposed—the forty-shilling freehold of Henry VI., or the payment of poor-rates, or the payment of a given rental, or even the possession of a bank book—were all purely artificial tests, and involved no principle whatever; "that *sometimes* ' drunkards, spend-thrifts, sluggards, vagrants, and profligates' lived in very good houses, and paid their rents and rates regularly." †

* Cox, *loc. cit.*   † Cox, *loc. cit.*, p. 122.

"Lord Robert Montagu said that the principle under which our liberties have taken root and grown up, is the theory that representation ought to depend on the possession of property; that land ought to be represented; because no stability nor permanence can be expected unless the electors have something at stake." *

This stubborn adhesion to lines of class, no matter how irrelevant to the purpose the basis of classification, is evidently a survival of the still more antique idea of caste. Equal rights were initiated at Rome, when privilege of property superseded privilege of birth; since the opportunity to acquire property was open, but the privilege of birth irreversibly closed. In its turn political privilege of property has been found oppressive, and its claims gradually relaxed.

"As *men*, those below the ten-pound line could have nothing to say; only as having money; and the acquisition of money and other value, was constantly being retarded by the fact that they were considered of less value than other men."

This for men. But for women is still reiterated and re-enforced the oldest, the most irreversible privilege of birth imaginable—the privileges of those born to one sex—over those who have been born to another.

* Cox, *loc. cit.*

Rights of Roman patricians, of Athenian eupatridæ, of Saxon thanes, of Norman nobles, of English whigs, even of ten-pound house-holders, have all been abrogated, or at least their supremacy abated. Only the one primi-tive right, the right of a circumstance of birth, which has been repudiated in such innumerable grants of other rights—this alone is maintained, because the persons wronged by it are unable to assert their own claims by force of arms, but must appeal to the reason and equity of those in power!

But to what else did the disfranchised classes of England appeal, in 1832, in 1867, and in 1884? Did they resort to arms? Did they excite—did they even threaten revolution? The peaceful triumph of their cause is an unerring harbin-ger of the success of the woman's similar claim. Their case is not indeed exactly identi-cal; but it is so closely analogous, that it is both fair and safe to reason from one to the other.

"A section of the press deprecated the ruinous effects of democracy in language which, read again after the Reform Bill of 1867, seems preposterous." *

"The great legislative and administrative period—per-haps the greatest in our annals—will be the history of

* Cox, *loc. cit.*

emancipation, political, social, moral, and intellectual. I consider my career as beginning with the Reform Act of 1832." *

The special contrast which the general enfranchisement of women in New York would offer to the English Reform Bills lies in the absolute numbers which would be involved. In England, Lord Russell's Bill of 1860 proposed the addition of only 248,000 persons to the electorate. In 1865 it was found that, in England and Wales, 488,920 persons were then entitled to vote. Of these, 128,603, or 26 per cent., maintained themselves by daily manual labor—were mechanics and artisans. Mr. Gladstone estimated that at that date the aggregate income of the working classes constituted $\frac{5}{12}$ of the total income of the country, and "yet they were put off with $\frac{1}{4}$ of the electoral power." The various detailed reforms proposed would add 400,000 persons to the electorate.

This number was almost equal to that of the whole number of voters already existing. In other words, the proposed bill of 1865 (which failed to become a law) would have almost "doubled the vote." By the bills of 1867 and

* Gladstone, letter to Midlothian Liberals, cited in *Evening Post*, March 27, 1894.

1884 the number of voters previous to 1865 has been quadrupled. (Cox).

In the State of New York, with a voting population of 1,500,000, the addition of 1,500,-000 would also double the vote. But it would do no more. And as, whatever our other difficulties have been, New York has experienced no more difficulty in handling and counting 1,500,000 votes than England had in casting 500,000, it may be presumed that with us 3,000,000 votes could be managed as easily as the 3,000,000 of the United Kingdom.* Further, the addition of women's votes would increase the proportion of the native, to that of the foreign, vote. In the State the total native-born population is 4,426,803, the foreign born 1,769,-649, or three times as many natives as aliens. There are 56,000 more native-born white females than native-born white males. They outnumber the foreign-born females by 1,430,345 throughout the State, and by 109,687 throughout the city.*

It has been constantly asserted during this year's suffrage campaign that the enfranchisement of women would only "double the exist-

* Taylor, *loc. cit.*, p. 616.
† Adele Fielde, *loc. cit.*

ing vote; and what was needed was to improve the quality, not increase the quantity, of the vote."* The Reform Bills of conservative England did exactly that—they "doubled the vote," and in the teeth of a frantic opposition which "protested" against an "increase in the quantity without security for improvement in the quality of the vote."

One of the great bugbears in England was the dread of a "monotonous constituency, a constituency whose predominant opinions would be identical, who would return to Parliament members holding the same ideas, the same opinions, the same sentiments."†

The same objection has been urged against the woman's vote, and even by members of the Massachusetts Senate. Because among public questions, the liquor question touches upon the interests of women, even while unenfranchised, it is assumed that they would think of nothing else, even after their admission to the general range of political discussion would have given them many other subjects for reflection.

On the other hand, the various differences which exist between the character or mental

---

* Protest of Brooklyn anti-suffragists.
† Disraeli, *Debates*, 1865, cited by Cox.

habit of women and of men, are alleged as liable to introduce dangerous confusion in a "mixed" electorate.

Such confusion has been foreboded by Gold-win Smith and others from "mixed colleges"; but the foreboding has remained as unsubstantial as an unpleasant morning dream. Certainly no American at this *fin du siècle* can venture to assert "homogeneity" is an essential condition of prosperous political life. Should he do so, he must in the same breath condemn his country, with brief delay, to overwhelming political disaster. Such a commingling of nationalities, races, languages, religions, traditions, habits, ideas, sentiments, and opinions, was never before known in any State. Under the Roman Empire these co-existed with each other, but only to a minimum extent co-operated to influence the Sovereignty of the State. Here they do both. This situation could only exist in a State both mighty, and entirely free.

The assertion that in such a heterogeneously composed community the addition of women voters would add a "disturbing element," is something like saying that a few thousand india-rubber balls dropped upon the moon would reverse the present relations of gravitation between that satellite and the earth.

However, to the extent to which it may be desirable to diminish the influence of the foreign conglomerate of nationalities and religions, the woman's vote is to be desired, since, as shown above, it would, at this time, increase the preponderance of the native vote; even, if that also be thought important, of the Protestant vote.

The peculiarity of the position of women is, and it is unique for any new class of voters, that they are not homogeneous with each other, but are so with the men among whom they live. Although some peculiarities of sex and training would emphasize in them certain tendencies of thought and action in preference to others, they would bring no distinctive ideas into the arena, but only those which were already common property of one or the other masculine group. The admission therefore would combine the advantages of both a homogeneous and a heterogeneous franchise, and at the same time would be free from the disadvantages of either.

The fourth question we have suggested may be presumed to especially refer to the ignorance of women, and to the lack of independence usually attributed to their sex.

The "anti-suffragists" of the drawing-rooms of Brooklyn and Albany have been ready to believe that when men objected to the female vote because it would increase the "ignorant vote," they only meant the ignorance of the maid servants in their kitchens, or of the female immigrants at Castle Garden. We women are under no such illusion. We are fully aware that this objection is a widely diffused conviction, sometimes expressed learnedly, sometimes elegantly, sometimes with extreme politeness and consideration, but always substantially identical with the offhand opinion of the average voter, who with feet on the mantelpiece, and hat well set on the back of his head, jerks his five-cent cigar out of his mouth long enough to ejaculate, "What do women know about politics, anyhow?" and then resumes his study of the sporting columns of the newspaper.

There is the ignorance of the educated woman and the ignorance of the ignorant woman, and they deserve a little different consideration.

The ignorance of otherwise educated women in regard to current politics certainly proves nothing against their intelligence. In the absence of any practical motive for acquiring information, such women could only study current politics in the same way as they would

study the structure of early Anglo-Saxon
societies, or the village communities of the
ancient Aryans; and some women have done
this very thing. But they were necessarily
those possessed of that surplus of intellectual
activity, which remains to a few people, and
unfortunately only a few, after all practical
functions of intelligence had been fulfilled.
What women would do with the practical
duties of political life, did these once devolve
upon them, must be judged by the intelligence
and efficiency with which they discharge the
duties they already assume. That those duties
are already multifarious and responsible no one
to-day would deny; and that women do acquit
themselves of these responsibilities with intelligence and fidelity, no one at present ventures
to dispute. Nothing can be much more fantastic than the idea that the new political duty
would add itself to those already assumed as a
"burden." Who ever can seriously make such
an assertion must speak from the bewilderment
of some troubled dream; a vision of Vathek,
where crowds of female shapes pace to and fro
in halls of Eblis, with hands on their palpi-
tating hearts, engaged at once in scrubbing,
cooking, sewing, teaching, talking, nursing the

measles, and pouring afternoon teas, chattering at the opera, shopping at Macy's, writing midnight copy for New York newspapers, studying the McKinley bill, *The Wealth of Nations*, and Mr. Atkinson's economic charts, following the investigations of the Lexow Committee and the inquiry into the sugar schedule, and conscientiously making up their minds in advance how they are going to vote for the next Presidential candidate, who has not yet been nominated!

The reasons that the alarm engendered by this vision is irrational, is that the vision itself is absurd, as it proves itself to be the moment its details are translated into masculine conditions. When people are doing one thing they are not doing another; when they engage in matters of larger concern they discover some way of condensing and handling more effectively affairs of lesser scope; where they require practical information for practical purposes, they divert, if necessary, some energies previously hitherto engaged in theoretical pursuits, and constituting a reserve force. Specifically, when women, newly enfranchised, should require either knowledge or advice in regard to voting, in addition to what they would require for themselves, they could, and would, follow the injunctions of St.

Paul to women admitted to the new sphere and new responsibilities of the Christian church, "ask their husbands at home."

After all, the most important effect of the suffrage is psychological. The permanent consciousness of power for effective action, the knowledge that their own thoughts have an equal chance with those of any other person, in being carried out by one's own will; this is what has always rendered the men of a free state so energetic, so acutely intelligent, so powerful. The influence of environment is only beginning to-day to be philosophically appreciated. It is just beginning to be suspected that the widely diffused ignorance of women is not a necessary organic peculiarity, but explicable by the fact that until recently they were forbidden to learn anything. Similarly we may inquire whether much of the observed practical feebleness of women, even in carrying out the thoughts they may have justly conceived, is not due to the social customs which, in such multiple directions, forbid their will to have any effect. The brain is not only the origin of activities, it is a result of them. When Laura Bridgman lost the power to see and hear, the part of her brain containing organs for sight and hearing atrophied, while the central convolutions, controlling the faculty of touch, developed out of all ordinary propor. tion. Life lies beyond the organs of life, but follows their shrinkage or expansion.

The ignorance of the ignorant women differs in no wise from that of ignorant men, except that it would be plausibly more amenable to legitimate influence.

We have already suggested that, with the overthrow of the boundary walls which now, theoretically and practically, tend to confine the interests of women to their respective "nests," and to isolate them from class interests in women, broad channels would be open for the overflow of the practical social enthusiasm so characteristic of women. In this direction we especially look for an answer to the fifth ques. tion we have raised, concerning the special public advantage which might result from the enfranchisement of women. We believe it would cause the liberation of innumerable molecular forces, which would disseminate themselves in all directions as civilizing agencies, acting upon small groups of people. Missionary work, Chinese Sunday-schools, blanket clubs, picnic festivals to raise money for the conversion of the heathen—the energies expended in such enterprises could be collected, raised, intensified, immensely fructified for good, when turned in the direction of instructing masses of ignorant women how to vote, so that the men chosen as policemen on their street, and the aldermen of their ward, and the police justices of their pre-cinct, should be competent, honest, and honor-able. Incidentally to such electioneering work, what other instruction would come; what ad-vantage from the commingling of classes on the true common ground of the public welfare where they can mingle; what enlightenment in regard to self-interests; what improvement in modes of living; what general uplifting of life!

That there would be no voting *en masse* at the dictate of party leaders, no submission to interested influence, no need, under the most stringent ballot laws, of perpetual vigilance against corruption and fraud, it would be absurd to deny. But these needs already exist; every motive for combating the evils peculiar to democratic societies, and which have succeeded to the evils of aristocratic societies, is fully aroused. The lateral extension of the franchise by the woman vote offers many suggestions of new resources against these old evils, and sug-gests no new evil itself. Numbers will be changed, and not proportions. He that is righteous will be righteous still, and possibly the converse will not be quite true. As before, in the words of Frederick Douglas, "we must trust all the knowledge of the community to take care of its ignorance, and all the virtue to take care of its vice."

Most interesting as a proof that the enfranchisement of women is simply an inevitable deduction from democratic principles, and irresistibly suggested by the actual conditions of our democratic republic, is the frequent recurrence of argument against woman suffrage, which turns out to be only argument in thin disguise against democracy. From much of the random talk which has flashed to and fro during this eventful spring, it might be inferred that plans had been submitted to the Constitutional Convention to change the government of our State to an aristocracy, or even to that most odious system of all—an oligarchy. It might be supposed that New York men and women had been invited to express their preference for the continuance of the existing system of social polity, where every one is represented, and the most energetic come to the front and finally rule; or rather for some system disinterred from the sepulchres of bygone centuries. Yet the only proposition for disfranchisement which has actually been submitted to the Convention came associated with the amendment to enfranchise women. In proposing this, Mr. Deane of Rochester also proposed " to disfranchise voters convicted of bribery."

Measures for disfranchisement are by no means unprecedented in Anglo-Saxon history. " The first recorded was passed in the eighth year of Henry VI., and limited the suffrage not only to freeholders, but to such of them as ' have free lands or tenements to the value of forty shillings, by the year at least, above all charges.' This was equivalent to a modern real property qualification of from thirty to forty pounds' annual value. It was never enlarged from the time of its imposition until the enactment of the Reform Bill of 1832. The same reactionary spirit which, before the close of the middle ages, thus brought about the disfranchisement of the landless freemen and the lesser freeholders within the shires, also impressed itself upon the municipal electoral system, producing a still more sweeping restriction of the franchise in the cities and towns. A persistent process of encroachment (on popular liberties) was inaugurated by the Tudors and pursued by the Stuarts ; and, under its influence, the English representative system ceased to be representative. . . . Of six hundred and fifty-eight members of the Lower House returned in 1816, four hundred and eighty-seven were the nominees of the government, and two hundred and sixty-seven private patrons,—one hundred and forty-four of the last-named being members of the House of Lords." *

Even the great Reform Bill of 1832, which transferred the control of the House of Commons from the landed aristocracy to the English middle classes, involved measures of disfranchisement co-relative with those which enfranchised newly developed interests. Fifty-six rotten boroughs of less than two thousand inhabitants were entirely disfranchised; thirty-two members were taken away from thirty-two boroughs having less than four thousand inhabitants.

In the United States, two measures of disfranchisement are already on record. The first was enacted in New Jersey, in 1807, and excluded from the suffrage the women propertyholders who had hitherto voted.

* Hannis Taylor, *loc. cit.*, p. 613.

" Nothing can be a greater mockery of this inalienable right of suffrage than to suffer it to be exercised by persons (women) who do not pretend to any judgment on the subject." *

The second measure was enacted most recently, and is embodied in the new State constitution of Mississippi, which now demands an educational qualification for the suffrage. The measure is intended to exclude from voting as many negroes as possible ; but in doing this a considerable number of white men are also disfranchised.

Thus it is absurd to declare, as has frequently been done, that the disfranchisement of classes once in possession of the suffrage is impossible. It has been accomplished, and not infrequently ; and, moreover, as an entirely peaceable measure, costing no bloodshed. The question involved is not practicability, but advisability. And certainly the history of England, from Henry VI. to William IV., does not show that "the encroachments" on the liberties of the people, in the interests of wealth and power, have proved anything but disastrous.

The desirable modifications of popular suf-

* *Errors and Omissions of the Constitution of New Jersey*, Emmons, Trenton, 1779. (Quoted in *History Woman Suffrage*, vol. i., p. 451.)

frage are not those which would annihilate, but which would educate, train, and refine this, and through more delicate and flexible adaptation of its present crude machinery render the suffrage more really representative. Real democracy is still in its infancy. The education of the (popular) Prince has hardly as yet advanced beyond the stage where ministers roll balls upon the floor for his amusement. The Dauphin has not yet found his Fenelon, nor Rasselas his sage. So little, however, does the enfranchisement of women stand in the way of the necessary education and evolution of democracy, that it is the fundamental contradiction to accepted ideas involved in the exclusion of women from the electorate, which is really one of the great stumbling-blocks in the way of reform. While half the adult, reasonable, important, influential, and interesting part of the population remains individually unrepresented, the importance of political representation wanes in popular appreciation. The crimes of usurpation of sovereignty, of defeating the popular will, of establishing the odious dominion of an oligarchy under the rule of the party boss—all cease to seem odious or to deserve any strenuous resistance, condemnation, or punishment. In a

State where education is free and so generally
sought after that compulsion is only occasionally
and locally required, illiteracy is a factor almost
negligeable, and of annually decreasing importance.   To-day, as always, it is not the mass of
the poor, but the combinations of the rich that
menace the State; not the labor organizations,
but the millionaire trusts which corrupt legislatures and administrations; not the workmen,
for whose employment the community appro-
priates a million dollars, but the officials who
squander or misappropriate the appropriation.
We may almost add—it is not the uninstructed
men who, on the confines of the civilization of
the community, sell their votes, who are chiefly
dangerous, but the instructed and adroitly intelligent men from the midst, who buy them; and
the other men, absorbed in private business or
political speculation, who wink at the process,
or fail to devise measures for its arrest.

On the 31st of May, the woman suffrage petition from New York was endorsed by leaders
of labor organizations, representing 100,000
men.   It is easy to assert, from within the stiff-
necked ranks of our metropolitan *bourgeoisie*,
that such endorsements forbode the utilization,
through pressure, threat, or purchase, of a new

contingent of feeble and dependent voters, to be massed according to party calculations, or to further schemes of hair-brained socialism. But the truth is, for those who desire the truth,— that such endorsements mean the distinct per-ception of and danger to the interests of work-ing men, of the unequal position of the great masses in their midst of working women. In the most obvious manner, and over and over again, has the readiness of women to accept lesser pay for the same work, undermined the strength of the combinations formed to secure a larger share of profits to labor. It would be ridiculous to pretend that political equality would enable women to earn as much as men wherever an actual inferiority in physical or mental strength compelled them to earn less. But in such cases the competition of women with men would do no harm, whereas now it is often as ruinous to men as their inability to command equal pay for equal work is injurious to themselves.

The existence and definite articulation of "Labor Questions," at which so many sneer,— simply marks the final transformation of the social system of militarism, into that of indus-trialism. It indicates that work is no longer held to be a mere incident in the social life of a community, whose serious business consisted in war, hunting, diplomacy, and conversation; but that in the social estimate as well as in fact, the productive forces of the community occupied the same relation to the life of the State, as the nutritive forces of the bodily organism to the individual life. That being thus fundamental to all social activities, and supporting all social existence, these nutritive forces of productive industry deserved all social respect; being indeed only justly subordinate to such social organs as correspond to the nerves, muscles, and brain of the animal body.

The share of women in political rights and life—imperfect, or deferred, or abrogated during the predominance of militarism—has become natural, has become inevitable, with the advent of industrialism, in which they so largely share. Useless therefore to assert the need of delaying enfranchisement to some other epoch of whose nature or occurrence no one has as yet the faintest conception.

Thus the precise advantages to the community to be anticipated from the enfranchisement of women, are to be inferred by any one capable of reasoning on the subject, from the entire trend of our argument which is now drawing to a close. It is not women, but men, and the heroic men of many generations, who have decided that a claim for Rights must, in the nature of things, antedate demonstrations of utility. If the highest utility in a democratic State be the development to the utmost of all the capacities of all its members; if the State suffers when energies, which might be usefully applied, are repressed, crippled, or allowed to rust; if interests suffer, when entrusted for their defence to any one but those directly concerned in them; if public morals suffer when the fundamental ideas of a given social order are traversed by conventions inconsistent with such ideas; if public ideals suffer when sovereign power, which should plainly devolve upon the highest attributes, is accorded to the lowest;—if all this be true, it is superfluous to try to show further that the enfranchisement of women would redound to the welfare of the Empire State. It is in this State, and almost in this alone, where may be discerned such steady line of historic sequence in the social advancement of women, as leads directly towards their political emancipation. Let the augury be fulfilled, and the line of march carried to its logical conclusion !

The remarkable phenomenon recently exhibited of the active opposition of women to such enfranchisement is, though interesting as a psychological and social phenomenon, of very little other significance. The extreme ignorance of the subject shown in the written protests; the naïve unconsciousness of the real reasons influencing much of the masculine protest, are natural to the inexperience of people who begin to talk volubly about what they themselves profess to have hardly ever thought. The gist of the opposition lies chiefly in the dread of innovation, which is a natural instinct with women,—an instinct intensified, moreover, by innumerable forces of tradition, training, and environment. Opposition to what is new, necessarily subsides so soon as the new has become the customary. The idea that the women who have shown so much public activity in voting against the suffrage petition, would refuse to go to the polls to defeat any other measure they might be opposed to, is evidently absurd. "The immense difficulty in democracies," it has been said, "lies in calling out the vote." Let the women try their hand!

"At present writing, the signatures to the suffrage petition number 300,000; the one anti-suffrage petition is signed by only 6000 persons."

The same publicists who have recently deprecated the popular desire to share in the
sovereignty, and attributed it to a mania for
"too much government," have, on other occasions, laid great stress on the difficulty of
managing the masses of a huge electorate, whose
members are so apt to be apathetic at elections.
The apathy may be taken as a measure, among
other things, of the influence of women, necessarily apathetic in regard to affairs from which
they are excluded, and in a position to infect
their "mates" with their own indifference. Our
naturalization laws are based on the postulate,
that the presence in the State of a vast mass of
aliens, indifferent to public affairs, and concentrated on their private interests, is a standing
menace to the public welfare. Why does not
the postulate apply to women, whose influence
is so much more extensive, subtle, and direct ?

Arguments to postpone the enfranchisement
of women are advanced by many who admit
the theoretical justice and expediency of the
measure. It is as difficult to detect any solid
grounds for such arguments as to estimate the
density of a morning mist.

"Among many arguments I have heard, the following
seems the most general, viz.: that had this rupture
happened forty or fifty years hence, instead of now, the

continent would have been more able to have shaken off the dependence. To which I reply, that our military ability *at this time* arises from the experience gained in the last war, and which in forty or fifty years' time would be totally extinct." *

Although the general evolution of women's condition during the last half century, and which puts them to-day in a position to claim political rights, cannot be compared in its effect with that of the French and Indian War; yet, in a certain sense, such comparison may be made with the share sustained by women in the anti-slavery struggle and the Civil War. Ground was gained then which since has been rather lost than further gained. We are constantly being told of the temporary " wave of the woman movement " which swept over the country coincidently with abolition-ism and teetotalism, and the Graham-bread gos-pel, and a host of other " isms." Because the Bloomer dress did not prevail (the gods were good!), it is readily assumed that the movement for human rights ended with the Fifteenth Amendment.

We are at present at the slack of the tide, no longer at the flood. Perhaps, however, already the ebb has begun to change !

* *Common Sense*, p. 115.

Let us at all events steadfastly resist the specious advice tendered from other quarters, to postpone our claim and wait till every one else has been served; wait, like poor Miss Flite, for the judgment which is likely only to come with the day of judgment. To wait till municipal politics are purified, minority representation secured, democracy grown from its crude beginnings; till illiteracy has ceased to exist; till venal votes have ceased to be bought and sold; till Catholics have ceased to struggle for the schools; till Protestants have ceased to imitate the bigotry of sixteenth century Catholics; till political rings have been dissolved; till the power of boss rule has been broken; till the liquor question has been eliminated from politics; till the Republican party has been raised to the level of Alexander Hamilton, and the Democratic party left at no lower eminence than Thomas Jefferson!

Is not this to say that political rights may be demanded only when political life shall have ceased to exist?

And now, lest the preceding pages may seem (as we hope,) to savor somewhat strongly of the passionate partisan flavor of their famous prototype, let us calm them down and close them in with the calm, pallid, bloodless, and therefore (we again hope,) utterly unobjectionable conclusions of a famous modern philosopher.

"Thus it has been shown that the rights of women must stand or fall with those of men, derived as they are from the same authority, involved in the same axiom, demonstrated by the same argument. That the law of equal freedom applies alike to both sexes has been further .proved by the fact that any other hypothesis involves us in inextricable difficulties. The idea that the rights of women are not equal to those of men has been abandoned as akin to the Eastern dogma that women have no souls. The position at present held by the weaker sex is of necessity a wrong one, seeing that the same selfishness which vitiates our political institutions must inevitably vitiate our domestic ones also. Proof has been given that the attitudes of mastery on the one side, and submission on the other, are essentially at variance with that refined sentiment which should subsist between husband and wife. The argument that married life would be impracticable under any other arrangement has been met by pointing out how the relationship of equality must become possible as fast as its justness is recognized. And lastly, it has been shown that the objections commonly raised against giving political power to women are founded on notions and prejudices that will not bear examination." *

"See! we might say, there is a general consciousness, a permanent Common Sense, independent indeed of each one of us, but with which we are, each one of us, in communication." †

* Herbert Spencer, *Social Statics*, 1871, p. 191. "The Rights of Women."

† Walter Pater, *Plato and Platonism*, p. 135.

APPENDIX.

ADDRESS ON BEHALF OF THE WOMEN OF THE CITY OF
NEW YORK

BEFORE THE

COMMITTEE ON SUFFRAGE OF THE STATE CONSTITU-
TIONAL CONVENTION,

May 31, 1894.

GENTLEMEN : It is with a deep sense of the momentous importance of our errand that we present ourselves
before you on this occasion.   Never in the history of the
world has a greater question been submitted to a deliberative body for discussion than that which we now pray
you to consider.   Other conventions, in this and other
lands, have framed constitutions for a State, have laid
down laws for a people, have enfranchised social classes,
have even called entire nations into being.   But we
ask you to consider that part of the State about which
constitutions have been silent ; to enfranchise a class so
immense that it constitutes the full half of all social
classes ; to call into political existence a vital half of
the nation, which hitherto, though personally, socially,
and legally recognized, has been, politically, non-existent.   Although we are only entitled to speak, and you

authorized to reply for a single State, it is certain that the enfranchisement of women in the State of New York would necessarily be followed, after no great lapse of time, by similar measures in all the other States of the Union. And further, as manhood suffrage in America has set an example which Europe has felt herself constrained to follow, so it is certain that the irresistible tendency to equalization of conditions among civilized nations would compel imitation in this particular also. And thus the enfranchisement of women in America would be the signal for the enfranchisement of women throughout the civilized world.

Momentous as would be this change, and far-reaching its consequences, it implies no sudden shock or overturning of established order, such as has attended political changes of far less importance and significance. We are well aware that this Convention is no revolutionary tribunal assembled to sap the foundations, or to overthrow the structure, of existing society. But the wise foresight which has imbedded in our State Constitution the provision for its own amendment every quarter of a century, admits by implication that in course of time, and in the orderly evolution of complex modern societies, new conditions are liable to arise, sufficiently serious to demand the modification of even our fundamental organic law. Such new conditions have arisen in the status of women.

Since 1846, when was framed the Constitution under which this State has since lived, immense changes have been effected in the industrial, legal, and educational status of women. The tremendous influence of untrammelled liberty of thought, in America, has brought about, not only an unrivalled degree of liberty for men, but a degree of personal liberty for women hitherto unparalleled. The tremendous activity of industrial expansion, has drawn women into the vortex of industrial life, so that they have become important and recognized factors in the wealth of the State.

In 1840, only half a dozen forms of employment other than household labor were open to women. In 1884 they were found employed in three hundred and fifty-four subdivisions of industries catalogued in the census. In 1892, it has been shown that there are few lines of remunerative employment not open to women. The United States Census of 1880 showed more than two and a half million women engaged in gainful employments And of these over 360,000 were so engaged in the State of New York.

We believe that a proper study of the facts of history shows that women have never been—as is sometimes asserted—a dependent class ; that even when confined to household labors, their work has been of a character and importance to as justly demand recognition by the State, as that of work carried on in the wholesale factories. In the great department of agricultural employments, that constitutes an entire fourth of all the industries enumerated on the census, the wives of the farmers bear a full share of the work of the farm, even though their work is not catalogued among the gainful occupations. Even when the men who furnish the raw material for their industry are the men of their own family—their fathers, husbands, or brothers,—the women who prepare the food, who make the clothing, and who keep in order the habitation of the men of the State, should be justly reckoned among its productive laborers, and not, as is commonly the case, assumed to be idlers, dependent on the bounty of relatives. When, however, the women, from choice or necessity, cross the threshold of their homes, and engage in distinctly non-domestic employments, no further illusion is possible as to their position. They have entered the ranks of industrial producers, have become independent contributors towards the wealth of the community, and are so recognized on the census. From this moment their distinct recognition as individuals by the State, as units in its body politic, entitled to an equal place with all other units discharging the same or equivalent functions, becomes an imperative necessity, a demand to be formulated alike by expediency, by justice, and by common sense. In a republican industrial community, those to whom such equal recognition is refused, fall out of the ranks of citizens, or never enter them. Whatever may be the personal privileges of their lot, whatever the legal protection accorded to their earnings, the public status of such a class remains strictly that of aliens. At the present moment this vast and constantly growing army of women industrials constitutes an alien class. The privation for this class of political right to defend its interests is only masked, but not compensated by its numerous inter-relations with those who have rights. The menace offered to the harmonious equilibrium of the State, by the presence in it of this alien class, is concealed by the peculiar physical weakness of its members, which renders them incapable of physical violence. But a menace may lie in a poison or a narcotic, as well as in a blow. Where—as in a demo-

cratic society is the case—it is necessary for every one
to be alert, vigilant, intensely awake, the apathy of aliens,
the indifference of aliens, the inability of aliens to unite
for the common good, is as dangerous as a dead-weight
clogging the wheels of delicate machinery. Women
industrials contribute to the wealth of the State, yet
often, through their relative helplessness, embarrass the
progress of their fellow-producers. Conscious of their
individual weakness, and ignorant of their strength in
combination, they are constantly liable to weaken the
strength of combinations made by those stronger than
themselves. Weakness kills force, for force can suffer
and die, but weakness desires to live. Innocent Deli-
lahs, the working women are often employed by the
Philistines to undermine the strength of the Labor Sam-
son. As perpetual minors, they should be entitled to
protection from the State. But the State is no foster-
mother ; it only protects those who can protect themselves ; and its last stretch of courtesy is reached when
it has put every one in a position to energetically demand
and secure their own protection.

It is not as industrials alone that women to-day occupy
important relations to the wealth of the State. They are
large holders of property, acquired either through their
own exertions, through gift, through marital right, or by
inheritance. It is estimated that throughout the State
women hold property in their own name to the amount
of at least five hundred millions of dollars. In the little
city of Rochester alone they pay taxes on twenty-nine
millions ; in the city of Brooklyn on a hundred and
three millions,—or twenty-two per cent. of all the tax-
able property of the city.

On this immense property women pay taxes, and yet remain unrepresented in the legislatures that apportion the taxation. It is not necessary to remind this Convention that from the beginning of history the question of taxation has constituted a continually recurring grievance. The equitable adjustment of taxation is one of the surest indications that a government is just and a people prosperous. The insistent demand of Anglo-Saxon people on both sides of the Atlantic, that no government shall tax a people, but that the people alone, through their representatives, shall tax themselves, has been a chief influence in securing for these peoples freedom, limitless expansion, and power. The only reason that it has been deemed just to tax women without representation is that, until very recently, women—that is at least those holding the normal position of their sex in marriage—have not really possessed their own property ; they have not been, in the eye of the law, persons.

Two years after the session of the Constitutional Convention in 1846, the Legislature of the State of New York, urged by the representations of Mrs. Stanton and other women working for suffrage, did for women in regard to the law the very thing we now pray this Convention to secure the means of doing in regard to political status—it made married women persons. The women, whose personality up to that precise date had been, in the language of the Common Law, "merged in that of their husbands," were then disengaged as distinct individuals. By a series of enactments extending from 1848 to 1862, a married woman became entitled to hold her property instead of being held by it : to administer it, to bequeath it by will, contract for it, to sue and be sued—in her own name,—to assume, in fact, all the responsibilities towards herself, her inheritance, her earnings, and finally her children, which belonged to a woman who had no husband to represent her, or to a man entitled, in law and in politics, to represent himself.

This Convention is thronged with lawyers, among the ablest in the State. We know that of all classes of men in the community, lawyers, from the very nature of their preoccupations and habitual lines of thought, must be the most conservative. Yet we appeal to them, as best fitted to answer, whether any change of statute or constitutional law, except those which emancipated slaves, could effect, or could imply, so complete a revolution in ideas, could determine so great a change in status, as that which made of women who had been legally non-existent, *persons*, with full legal and individual responsibilities ?

It will be as logical for this Convention to complete the legislation of 1848 by now equalizing the political rights of women, as it was for the French Revolution of 1848 to confer political rights upon the men who had become equal before the law in 1793.

The industrial work of women, the possession of inherited wealth, the legal emancipation, and enforced assumption of responsibility, would all have been inadequate without correlative improvement in the education of women. So rapid has been this improvement, so generally is now accepted the claim of women to the highest education, that it is often forgotten in how recent times women were refused access to even the lowest. Less than a hundred years ago, in this State and in New England, girls were excluded from even the elementary public schools ; or, when admitted, untaught even in arithmetic ; or, when this began to be conceded, allowed to learn addition, but forbidden to proceed to the three other rules. Not until 1821 was a high school open for women, and that was at Troy, New York.

This State has taken the lead, not only in legislation for women, but in the education of women. In 1865 the first institution claiming to confer collegiate instruction was founded by Matthew Vassar at Poughkeepsie. Up to 1890, nine hundred graduates had left this one institution. In 1872, women were admitted to the great Cornell State University at Ithaca. In 1875, a New York millionaire made his initial gift of $250,000 for the residence of women students at Cornell. In 1889, Barnard College received its official sanction and grant of affiliation from the Trustees of Columbia College—one of the oldest universities in the United States,—and in 1893 a class of girls thence received their academic diplomas together with the Columbia students.

In 1849 the first woman physician, Elizabeth Blackwell, received her diploma at Geneva. The first hospital in the world to be conducted by women physicians, the New York Infirmary, was founded by Elizabeth Blackwell in 1857, and its Medical College secured a legal charter from the State in 1867. The great medical societies of the county and State of New York were almost the first to officially recognize women physicians, and put an end to an arduous struggle for equal rights, which resembles point by point that which is now going on to secure equal political rights. Nor have the activities of educated women been confined to this one sphere of professional or public work. The Normal Schools of

Albany, New York, and Oswego have trained several generations of teachers, to whose hands is now mainly entrusted the primary and secondary education of the youth of both sexes throughout the State. Through the public press women share in increasing numbers and with increasing influence in moulding public opinion. During the civil war the women of this State were among the foremost in the patriotic work of aiding, encouraging, and practically caring for the soldiers of our armies. A New York woman and veteran philanthropist, Abby Hopper Gibbs, directed hospitals on the Potomac. The Sanitary Commission originated in a parlor conference called by a New York woman, Dr. Elizabeth Blackwell, and during four years consumed the energies of hundreds of New York women under the lead of one whose name is historic—Louisa Lee Schuyler.

In 1873 a group of New York ladies, headed by Miss Schuyler, organized the State Charities Aid Association, and inaugurated reform in the administration of the hospitals, almshouses, prisons, and insane asylums throughout the State. In 1876, in partial recognition of the value of this work, Governor Tilden appointed one of the members of the Association—Josephine Shaw Lowell—as a member of the State Board of Charities, the first official appointment ever made to a woman in this State. In 1887 the Mayor of the City of New York appointed two women to serve on the School Board; and in 1892 a large number of women were sent as official delegates from New York to the Woman's Board of the World's Fair.

In perfectly natural sequence to all these manifestations of professional and social activity on the part of

women, and as a possibly unconscious recognition of the
value of this activity for the welfare of the State, the
Legislature in 1888 threw open to women the profession
of law. This is the profession whose exercise stands so
closely related to political prerogative that, in both
Italy and Belgium, women, though admitted to medicine, have been recently refused admission to the bar,
on the ground that they must be disqualified for this
profession so long as they remained deprived of political
rights.

In the State of New York the necessity for the franchise as an indispensable preliminary to the exercise of
public functions presumed to be suitable for women,
has been judicially affirmed in another connection. The
Supreme Court, late in the year 1893, decided that the
law passed in 1880 permitting women to vote for School
Commissioner was unconstitutional, and that women
could not exercise an influence nor have a voice in the
public schooling of their own children, until they should
have been empowered to do so by means of a constitutional amendment.

This decision has become the incident to precipitate
the whole discussion of woman suffrage within the range
of immediate practical issues. We believe that future
ages will class it with that famous levy of illegal ship-
money, whose resistance by John Hampden laid the
modern foundation for the liberties of England.

It was impossible, in face of the immense evolution of
the status of women, personal, industrial, legal, educational, and social, not to suggest their practical participation in one affair which so immediately concerns
women, namely, the schooling of children. In New

York City alone are over three thousand female teachers. It seemed impossible to hold longer to the doctrine that where so many women had been deemed capable of the expert work involved in teaching, none should be qualified, none should have the right to a voice in the selection of the officers who were to superintend the teaching. Yet this contradiction, deemed impossible by the universal common-sense of the community, has been pronounced entrenched in all the authority of the law by the Supreme Court. And it is very well that it should be so. The contradiction which pronounces unfit to vote, the women who have been solemnly ordained fit to teach, is hardly more flagrant than that now embodied in the laws of. twelve States of the Union, which declares that women may elect officers to the school board, but may not exercise any other right of suffrage.

It is in the line of march which the thought of this State has pursued for the last fifty years to declare that all exercise of public function,—all expression of public choice—is an act of sovereignty, and can only be performed by those who have been empowered for such acts.

The issue is thus most distinctly, most authoritatively stated. At the very moment that the women of this State have reached a degree of development, have demonstrated a social capacity, absolutely unknown until the present half century ; at the very moment when, coincidently, the enlargement of the franchise has brought into the electorate classes also hitherto unknown ; that same moment is chosen in which to reduce women to a degree of political inferiority which is also absolutely unprecedented.

No political experiment is more recent, has had so far a shorter span of duration, than that of universal manhood suffrage. Only little by little have been abolished the restrictions of church membership, of education, and of modest property qualification, which formerly prevailed throughout the United States. The farthest limit of possible extension of masculine franchise was reached when, at the close of the Civil War, the right of suffrage was bestowed on the newly emancipated slaves.

Until, practically, to-day the inequalities of political rights have been along lines of social class distinction. The well-born, the powerful, the educated, the rich, have ruled. The poor, the ignorant, the helpless have submitted. Macaulay declares that the upper and middle orders are the natural representatives of the human race. Whether advisably or not, it is they who have been the representatives. Thus it has happened that women, though unenfranchised, and submitted to the personal sovereignty of the men of their own families and own class, have enjoyed superiority to and even actual supremacy over thousands of men in lower classes. But to-day, for the first time, classes have been indistinguishably fused; all previous lines of cleavage have been consolidated into one great line of demarcation, which makes a political class out of a sex. For the first time, all political right, privilege, and power reposes undisguisedly on the one brutal fact of sex, unsupported, untempered, unalloyed by any attribute of education, any justification of intelligence, any glamour of wealth, any prestige of birth, any insignia of actual power. For the first time, all women, no matter how well born, how well educated, how intelligent, how rich, how serviceable to the State, have been rendered the political inferiors of men, no matter how base-born, how poverty-stricken, how ignorant, how vicious, how brutal. The pauper in the almshouse may vote, the lady who devotes herself to getting that almshouse made habitable may not. The tramp who begs cold victuals in the kitchen may vote ; the heiress who feeds him, and endows a university may not. Communities are agitated and Legislatures convulsed to devise means to secure the right of suffrage to the illiterate voter. And the writers, journalists, physicians, teachers, the wives and daughters and the companions of the best educated men in the State, are left in silence ; blotted out, swamped, obliterated behind this cloud of often besotted ignorance. To-day, the immigrants pouring in through the open gates of our seaport towns—the Indian when settled in severalty,—the negro hardly emancipated from the degradation of two hundred years of slavery,—may all share in the Sovereignty of the State. The white woman—the American woman, —the woman in whose veins runs the blood of those heroic colonists who founded our country, of those women who helped to sustain the courage of their husbands in the Revolutionary War ; the woman who may have given the flower of her youth and health in the service of our Civil War—this woman is excluded. To-day women constitute the only class of sane people excluded from the franchise, the only class deprived of political representation, except the tribal Indians and the Chinese.

Sirs : We dare to assert that this is a monstrous anomaly; and further, though commonly supposed to continue an immemorable tradition, is really an immense innovation on all systems of hitherto existing order. It is an anomaly which of itself suffices to explain much of the dangerous vulgarization of political ideal which has lately been noticed among us,—much of the fashionable contempt which is beginning to be expressed for Popular Sovereignty. It is possible for a Sovereign to have defects, vices, and yet retain respect. But the suspicion of a base birth, or an illegitimate origin, suffices to cover him with ignominy. Until now, the exclusion of women from the Sovereignty has been justified by the fear that their immense inferiority would infuse a contemptible weakness into the body politic. But to-day, the one form of strength of which women are deprived, is the very form which has ceased to be essential for the purpose. Necessary for pugilistic contests, which are forbidden by law, it is irrelevant to the qualifications of those who either administer or vote for a government founded on opinion. Conversely, the form of strength which *is* so greatly needed in the counsels of the Republic, "the reason firm, the temperate will, endurance, foresight, patience, skill," are adjudged by the highest authority to be the natural dower of thousands of women. Where, then, does the legitimacy of the Sovereignty lie,—with the thousands who have the power without the necessary qualification, or with those other thousands who have the qualifications but are forcibly excluded from the power?

So lax in these facile days has become the conception of power, so loose and confused the Idea of Sovereignty, that we are often advised not to press our claim, because it really makes no difference who rules. Because, it is said, in a democracy, sovereignty is so minutely subdivided that the infinitesimal crumbs which fall to each

man's portion are not worth scrambling for. But we refuse to think of the Republic as a barnyard filled with
insignificant fowl! If the right to rule has been removed
from certain men on account of their inadequacy, it has
been transferred to Man, and to such part of the human
race as can by their strength of soul make good its claim
to such lofty right. Of such humanity we are a part.
And while among those to whom at present is exclusively entrusted the power are thousands, admitted on all
sides to be unworthy of it, there are among us thousands
of women intrinsically fitted for those functions of citizenship which can only by an eclipse of political faith
be despised.

Capacity to bear arms, in fulfilment of military duty,
is not, in the State of New York, reckoned among the
necessary qualifications of voters. Nor indeed has such
capacity ever sufficed to confer a share in the sovereignty. The feudal knights of the middle ages exercised some sort of suffrage,—but the men-at-arms who followed them to battle did not. The Duke of Cambridge,
Commander-in-chief of the British Army, has—like his
predecessors for six hundred years, been able to vote.
But, until the other day, the men who make up the army
and do the fighting had no vote, and many of them
are still unenfranchised. Even in France and Germany,
where for a few years universal manhood suffrage has
existed, and universal military duty has been revived,
the right of suffrage and the duty of bearing arms are
not coterminous. There, as here, men over forty-five,
the only sons of widows, teachers, clergymen, physicians,
men affected with slight bodily infirmities, are exempt
from military duty in the field, but are not therefore

deprived of the right of suffrage at home. In our State, even the universal training for arms is dispensed with ; no conscription exists ; and the only occasion on which men can be actually compelled to fight, is in the case of a war of such magnitude as necessitates a draft in excess of the contingents furnished by volunteers. In the entire course of our history, since the landing of the Pilgrims or the settlement of New York, such a war has arisen once !

We do not live in the midst of an armed camp like France and Germany ; we, like our English kindred, reserve our war forces for the day when they shall be really needed. During the interval, we are an industrial community, with a government of the people, for the people, and by the people, a government professedly and actually founded on Public Opinion. The will of the majority rules, for the time being, not because, as has been crudely asserted, it possesses the power, by brute force, to compel the minority to obey its behests ; but because, after ages of strife, it has been found more convenient, more equitable, more conducive to the welfare of the State, that the minority should submit, until, through argument and persuasion, they shall have been able to win over the majority.

Now that this stage in the evolution of modern societies has been reached, it has become possible for women to demand their share also in the expression of the Public Opinion which is to rule. They could not claim this while it was necessary to defend opinions by arms ; but this is no longer either necessary or expected. They could not even claim a place among the authorized factors of Public Opinion, so long as, in the universal judgment of the world, women had no opinions, and could have none worth having. But this is no longer believed. The moment therefore has at last arrived when, in an Industrial Society, whose conflicts have become those of ideas, and whose arts the arts of peace, women may, with equal justice and decorum, come forward to claim a place among the other powers of the earth. Should war actually arise, the fact that the political action of women had been added to that of the non-combatant forces of society, could surely do nothing to weaken the strength of the forces which were actually enlisted to fight.

We do not admit that exemption from military duty is a concession of courtesy, for which women should be so grateful as to refrain from asking for anything else. The military functions performed by men, and so often perverted to most atrocious uses, have never been more than the equivalent for the function of child-bearing imposed by nature upon women. It is not a fanciful nor sentimental, it is an exact and just equivalence. The man who exposes his life in battle, can do no more than his mother did in the hour she bore him. And the functions of maternity persist, and will persist to the end of time,—while the calls to arms are becoming so faint and rare that, three times since the Revolutionary War, an entire generation of men has grown up without having heard them.

If children are desired in households to make the happiness of their parents, none the less are they needed in the State of which they are to become the citizens. Those therefore who bear and rear them do most certainly perform a social function, and one of transcendental importance. All social events, all political action, converge ultimately upon these households and affect these children. How then can it be fitting, that such political action, framed as we know it to be by the dictates of Public Opinion, should remain officially uninfluenced by the mothers of the State ? How can it be just that those mothers themselves remain within the body politic as aliens, their will unrepresented, their personalities nonexistent ? To affirm that this is of no consequence, to pretend that these women are virtually represented because laws protect their property, and because they may be defended against personal violence, is simply to recur to the state of opinion which prevailed when the personality of the married women was, in truth, merged, absolutely submerged, before the law. Before 1848, the affirmation was logical and consistent. To-day it is inconsistent,—a futile anachronism.

To-day is certainly favorable to the treatment of women with kindness, consideration, and even respect. The moment is, however, less propitious to the discussion of their rights, for all interest in the question of rights seems, for the moment, to have flagged. For the first time in a hundred and fifty years there is a lull in the mighty series of conflicts which have been waging so successfully to secure human rights. The lull in the interest is chiefly due to the success of the struggle. So many rights have been conquered that it seems to many as if all had been gained. Worse,—because some roseate hopes have been disappointed,—we are sometimes told that nothing has been gained. We are sometimes told that democracy is a failure ; that universal suffrage is a curse ; that the very conception of Rights, conception the most powerful, the most majestic, the most awful which has ever dominated the world, is a mere abstraction, as useless as bodiless ; a schoolboy sophism, a schoolgirl metaphor concocted to conceal a vacuum of thought. A little further, and we shall be told that our Revolutionary War was sordid ; that the French Revolution was the clamor of a drunken mob ; that the Revolution of 1848 was a mere paradox of metaphysicians ; and the emancipation of American slaves a gigantic mistake due to the blind recklessness of a victorious party !

When the thoughts of men have for the moment so generally declined to this dull level, it is well that they should have been suddenly uplifted again by the high errand of this Convention. The moment has again recurred when the people must preoccupy themselves with the fundamental doctrines on which repose the entire framework of their social structure. It is then seen, and will be seen again every quarter of a century, that there is nothing more fundamental in a given social order than its conception of Rights. What *is* the right thing to be done ? whose rights may have been defrauded ; how rights may in the future be better maintained ;—these are the very questions which are to absorb the energies and preoccupy the gravest thought of this deliberative body throughout the summer.

Our Constitutional Conventions only meet once in twenty years ; but the problem of Rights is of no such intermittent recurrence. It recurs all the time,—daily ; it is involved in every transaction effected between human beings, at home or abroad, in business or in politics, in national issues, in municipal difficulties, in family dissensions. Rules for the solution of this problem are expounded every week in the churches, and laid down every day in the law courts. No personal or social ideal is possible without a conception of rights, and every lofty character manifests its superiority to the herd, by the clearness with which it recognizes the existence of rights, and by the unflinching tenacity with which it insists upon their maintenance.

Hence the danger, the vast and subtle danger, of so educating one half the population of a free State, that it has no vivid conception of Rights. Why should we wonder at the low tone which habitually prevails at present in relation to public affairs, when the women who stand as guardians at the fountain sources and household shrines of thought are trained to believe that there are no Rights, but only Privileges, Expediences, Immunities ? Can those who cower before the public ridicule which greets the enunciation of the Rights of Women ; who are habituated to stifle generous impulses for their own larger freedom at the authoritative dictation of the men they see in power,—can such women be relied upon to nerve the nation's heart for generous deeds ?

When the question of women's right to a direct share in the popular sovereignty had not been raised ; when political rights were restricted to certain social classes, proudly tenacious of their privileges, it was then possible for women also to share the pride, and, unconscious of their individual subordination, to lend the strength of their influence to inspiring their men. It was possible for Volumnia to calm the blind fury of Coriolanus ; it was possible for Cornelia to train the patriotic fervor of the Gracchi. But this time has past. For good or for ill, the question of the Rights of Women has been raised, and will not down. It has taken its place among the claims of all disenfranchised classes, and will not be excluded. If any question of rights be fundamental, this also is fundamental. If confusion of ideas and apathy be ever-dangerous, here also it is disastrous.

It is easy to assert, it is impossible to prove that we sophistically pervert the principles of democratic government when we claim that these apply to our case also. It is easy to say in two breaths—for it has been reiterated in one—that women's right to the suffrage is not implied in democracy, and that democracy, after fifty years of trial has proved such a failure, that its principles must now, in any case, be abjured. How can democracy prove other than a failure when the citizens of a free State cease to believe in it ! How can the illiterate vote become other than a danger when the educated voter abstains from exercising over it his just and natural ascendancy? How can political affairs move among large issues, if the only ideas which are abroad, which are respected, are fatally small? What other alternative is there to Public Right, but Private Greed ? If it be only a question of supposed expediences,—what can seem more expedient to every man than to fill his own pocket, accumulate his own illicit fortune,—and retreat to whence he had never emerged,—the underground cellar of his private life ?

Thus it is that, although we believe our demand to be fully in accord with public utility, and to meet some of the most serious wants of the time, we should be false to our trust did we rest this claim primarily upon expediency.   We hope to show that the concession of suffrage to woman will be practically useful in innumerable directions ; but we should unworthily belittle our case did we seek to introduce it on the ground that it could be made subservient to anything else.   We demand the suffrage as a Right—not in a metaphysical sense,—but because we do fulfil all the essential conditions which the State has proclaimed necessary to qualify for the electorate. We demand it, because to-day, and not a thousand years ago,—because in the State of New York, and not in France or Germany or Austria,—women are recognized by law and custom to be persons, and to possess intelligence entirely equal to the average intelligence of those who already exercise the suffrage.   We demand it, on no new principle, but on the double principle which runs through all our institutions, namely : that all the intelligence in the State must be enlisted for its welfare, and that all the weakness in the community must be represented for its own defence.   There are women among us of intelligence, of wealth, of leisure, of high character, who only demand the opportunity to serve the State nobly, as they have already shown their ability to promote the welfare of the community in public affairs. And there are other women among us—hard-working, patient, industrious,—who require the suffrage, and the opportunities of the suffrage, and the immense practical education of the suffrage, to enable them to better advance the interests of their own affairs.   And there are poor and weak women among us, defenceless except so far as they may be touched by an occasional enthusiasm of philanthropy, who require the status of a definite representation—a medium through which they can make their wants known—which shall do for them, as the suffrage alone has been able to do for other masses of the poor and weak : give them means to defend themselves, enable them to take the initial step in rising out of otherwise easily-forgotten misery. In a community where the definition of a social unit is the person who casts one vote, every one who casts no vote is reckoned as less than a unit,—and hence suffers in the social estimate and in her own. Her power for work is lessened, and its recompense correlatively diminished.

It is to these same poor and working women that objection is most often made when we demand equal suffrage, and when we embrace in our demand all classes of women,—*because* the suffrage is now exercised by all classes of men. It is said that these women, adding an inherent weakness of sex to the weaknesses of ignorance and poverty, will be, even more than the men of their families, subject to corrupt influence, liable to be induced to sell their votes to the party, or even to the private agents, who will offer the highest price for them. It is even whispered that there is, in large cities, a class of women, whose names dare not be mentioned out loud, who would be solidly voted by the police,—and that *therefore* all the honest and virtuous women of the State must remain disfranchised ! Was ever covert insult so distinctly offered to American womanhood !

It has been proposed, on other occasions, to accord special legal recognition to these unfortunate women : to subject them to a slavery even more stringent than that in which they are now bound : to record their names upon the municipal archives, not in order that their defencelessness might be represented, but so that the men who are their accomplices in degradation might be protected. Other women, from the shelter of happy and honored homes, have successfully resisted this iniquitous proposal, and no such archaic infamy as yet stains the legislature of this State. But do not these facts, does not the prompt reference to such conditions, the moment a demand arises for political freedom, and political representation for women, itself indicate the ultimate outcome, the last and darkest effect, of the general social inequality of women?

We fully believe that the great reason why the lot of masses of toiling women is so miserable, is because on the one hand women have never been accustomed to band together for self-development and self-protection; and on the other hand, because women enjoying personal protection have not been accustomed to think of the affairs of masses of women and children as their especial concern. The assumption still holds in theory, though daily contradicted by facts,—that all the concerns of women are adequately provided for by the solicitude of their own families. Yet it is perfectly well known, that society was obliged to enact laws to protect the women and children working in factories; not only against the greed of the employers of the so-called enlightened classes, but against the brutal insistence of the husbands and fathers who tried to work them to death.

In theory, women are always protected at home. In fact, laws are constantly being required for their special protection. Why is it desirable to leave such legal or social protection to be secured, if at all, by tedious and roundabout methods,—through petitions, and through the efforts of other people, whose warmest enthusiasm can hardly ever equal the energy of those who speak for themselves ? Why should not the women have the right to speak for themselves, and by their own mouths to make their own wants known ?

Herein lies the true solution of the problem of the illiterate vote. The influence of the women who are now busily engaged in civilizing the hordes of uncivilized people in our midst, will be utilized, not only to kindle the lagging interest of the men of their own class, but to so guide ignorant women voters, that they could be made to counterbalance, when necessary, the votes of ignorant and interested men. Here is a broad channel for the missionary enthusiasm of women, now too often allowed to run to waste in the sands of foreign heathendom. Success in such direction is rendered possible by the secrecy of the ballot, which the persistent efforts of public-spirited men have secured. Every effort to improve the purity of the ballot facilitates the participation of women in the suffrage. It is an omen of splendid augury that this very Committee before which our amendment is brought, is also charged with the grave duty of devising measures for the better protection of the ballot. We could ask no better introduction to the voters of this State for the cause of Equal Suffrage, than such intimate, such inseparable association with the cause of Purity of the Suffrage.

In bringing this cause of Equal Suffrage before this Convention, we are supported by the approval of thousands of men and women, who join us, because they believe either that the demand is just, or that it is timely, or that it is favorable to their own interests, or that it is ultimately conducive to the best interests of the State. Confessedly, however, the demand does not receive unanimous support. Did it do so, it would be irresistible, while we are aware that the success of our petition is trembling in the balance. But a unanimous demand for anything would also be unprecedented to the point of the miraculous.

Not all who fail to support us are to be counted among our really obstinate opponents. There are many who applaud the participation of women in public affairs, but who maintain that they have done such good work without the ballot, it is useless to confer this upon them. This view is too inconsistent to deserve commentary. More solid is the objection of those who distinctly dislike the participation of women in public affairs. There are thousands who still maintain the immemorable tradition, that the world is destined to remain forever divided into two great classes—the men to go out in the world, the women to stay at home within the house. These confound the historic origin of conditions with the permanent law of conditions. They are so pleased with women in their differentiation from men, that they dread any change which may seem to approximate them to men. To apply to the case of women, the same ideas of Rights, the same measure of liberties, the same rules for activities, which they accept for men, seems to such minds almost blasphemous, and revolting alike to the most elementary instinct, and to the most obvious common sense.

We certainly do claim, however, that women, however physically different, are, mentally and morally, *not* essentially different from men. That the differences in

as persons; and the right and responsibility to guard
the persons and the inheritance of their children; they
are given a right to maintenance to the extent to which
their own industrial capacity is lessened by the care of
their children; and in view of this, they are constrained
to follow the domicile of their husbands so long as he
acquits himself of his own responsibility.

We do believe that this special relation of women to
children, in which the heart of the world has always felt
there was something sacred, serves to impress upon
women certain tendencies, to endow them with certain
virtues which not only contribute to the charm which
their anxious friends fear might be destroyed, but which
will render them of special value in public affairs. Their
conservatism, their economy, their horror of waste, their
interest in personal character, the very simplicity of
their judgment, their preoccupation with direct and
living issues, are all qualities generated by the special
circumstances which have surrounded women, and must
continue to surround them. These can not be broken
down by the fact of sharing the suffrage, for they lie far
deeper than any political condition; they exist in the
very nature of things.

A single phrase, often, but none too often repeated,
sums up this aspect of the case. To the extent to which
women resemble men, they require the same liberties;
to the extent to which they differ, they require their own
representation, and the State requires their special influence. Under the new, the extremely new régime of
universal manhood suffrage, the State has become like a
mining camp on the frontier. We claim that it should be
re-constituted as a household, where, if man is at the

head, for the protection and the defence, woman shall have her equal place as the mother, the daughter, the caretaker, the administrator, the conserver. We do not propose, after all, to change the existing sphere of women. Political status reflects and sanctions social change—it cannot create it. Political activities may become an occupation—but not political rights. How many women would engage in politics were they so empowered—how many would accept office, were they elected, it is impossible to foresee, and it is absolutely useless to discuss. We are not here to seek privileges for a few—but equal opportunity for all. We are not here to demand the maximum responsibilities in the gift of the State, but only the minimum rights. If women engage to-day in a hundred pursuits outside their households, it is not the suffrage which is the cause of this, for they do not possess the suffrage. The same causes, industrial and intellectual, which have led to a social expansion which is almost a revolution, will continue to operate ; but the suffrage, while it will not weaken, can hardly intensify their influence. Women will not be sent into a new place by possession of the ballot. Like men, they will vote in the places where they already stand—in the mart, the factory, the place of business ; but also in the schoolroom, the library, the hospital, and—far more often than all—in the household. If, in capacity, taste, and opportunity, women have in this half century, approximated towards the capacities of men, it is not in order to be men that they now desire to vote. It is because they are—and are fully satisfied to be—women.

Because they are women, and yielding, and ready to give way to others, the friends of this cause have been beset, not only by its opponents, but by many half-hearted friends. "Your demand is just," these say, "but it should not be made at this time. The times are too critical ; there are too many things must be done first. Municipal politics must be purified ; minority representation must be secured ; democracy must grow from its first crude beginnings ; illiteracy must cease to exist ; venal votes must cease to be bought and sold ; Catholics must cease to struggle for the schools ; Protestants must cease to imitate the bigotry of sixteenth-century Catholics ; political rings must be dissolved ; the power of boss rule broken ; the liquor question eliminated from politics ; the Republican party be raised to the level of Alexander Hamilton, and the Democrats left at no lower eminence than that of Thomas Jefferson. When all these things shall come or shall have been accomplished— then, and not till then, may women, who really entertain a just and patriotic concern for the public weal, prefer their claim, and modestly demand the suffrage."

Is not this to say that political rights may be demanded only when political life shall have ceased to exist ?

This request to delay—this specious appeal to the disinterestedness of women—is the same dangerous compliment proffered in 1867 by Horace Greeley on behalf of the negro, and a few years ago by Mr. Gladstone to the women of England on behalf of Home Rule.

Who, entrenched in an accorded privilege, ever regarded the claims of those outside as other than unimportant, insignificant, visionary ? We are told now that the common sense and love of justice of all civilized countries applaud all efforts to secure for women their individual public rights ; to remove from these all previous restriction ; but that legislators still obstinately and justly refuse the concession of political rights. But fifty years ago these legal and other public rights were everywhere refused with the same obstinacy, and with exactly the same arguments.

No social sphere is more remote from political life than that of medicine ; and none, it might be imagined, more appropriate to women. Yet, in all the European countries of two hemispheres, language was racked to find words, and science tortured to find arguments sufficiently abusive to condemn the proposal to allow women to minister to children and to the sick of their own sex. We are perfectly well aware that industrial and professional competition are entirely different matters from Popular Sovereignty. But when we find the same instincts aroused, the same opposition excited, the same arguments advanced, and the same determination manifested, by trades unions to exclude women from trades ; by learned societies to exclude them from professions ; by universities to exclude them from learning ; and by voters to exclude them from the polls, we cannot avoid asking whether the difference in the cases is not balanced by the identity in the mental attitude of the opponents.

The time to press the demand for a right is that when some one has been found to voice the demand. Since 1848 there have not been lacking women—women like Mrs. Stanton and Lucy Stone—who passed from abolition conventions to the Legislatures of their own States, there to urge the claims of equal suffrage. There have not been lacking women who have worked as persistently,—and, in comparison with the opportunities afforded, as greatly,—for the enfranchisement of their sex, as O'Connell worked for the liberties of Ireland, or Mazzini for those of Italy.

All the reforms in the legal position of women, and much of their educational advancement, have been due to the impulse given by the women who were working for the suffrage ; and to them also is indirectly due much of the industrial emancipation.

Still, all women do not demand the suffrage. We are sometimes told that the thousands of women who do want the suffrage must wait until those who are now indifferent, or even hostile, can be converted from their position.

Gentlemen, we declare that theory is preposterous. It is true that the exercise of an independent sovereignty necessitates the demonstration of a very considerable amount of independence. A rebel state that cannot break its own blockade may not call upon a foreign power to move from its neutrality to do so. But the demand for equal suffrage is in nowise analogous to a claim for independent sovereignty. It is rather analogous to the claim to the protection of existing laws, which any group of people, or even a single person may make, who believes himself to have been wronged in sentiment, person, or property. Claims for the enforcement of existing laws, for the application to new cases of principles embodied in previous laws, for the amendment of existing institutions, are never preferred by the whole community, or an entire class, or the majority of a class, or even by a large minority. The bugbear that women in voting would always band together as a class, should be sufficiently dissipated by the fact that even now, when a most distinctly class issue is presented—

since it affects the disabilities of all women,—women are not a unit in their opinion upon it. So great is the mental isolation engendered in a class politically non-existent, that many women profess even now never to have thought of the franchise. Others, educated in a lifetime of indifference to public affairs, remain absolutely indifferent. Others, accustomed to defer to masculine opinion, submit at the first breath of ridicule from masculine friends. Others, believing themselves independent thinkers, yet fall an easy prey to the first sophism spread for innocent and unwary feet. Others, sincerely alarmed at any innovation of existing order, content with their own lives and with things as they are, shrink from the suggestion of change, and dread the unknown. Others, with the instinct for public activities and intellectual interests already satisfied, do not imagine how political privilege could improve their own situation, and fail to inquire whether it could improve that of other women. Others are not ashamed to feel and express all the concentrated bitterness of aversion to equal rights, establishing common bonds between themselves and social inferiors, which privileged classes have always expressed when called upon to extend, to share the Sovereignty. Men have resisted the demand for the enfranchisement of other men ; it is no miracle, therefore, that women resist a similar demand for women.

There have always been found individuals ready to uphold the claims of a social class to which they either belonged or wished to be thought to belong, and this even at the expense of their own permanent interests. Professional men were found in France to uphold Guizot in refusing a vote to the professions. The poor white laborers of the South sustained the planters in defending slavery, the institution which condemned labor to ignominy.

We believe that the suffrage is in the ultimate interests of all women, as it has been of all men ; but we do not expect all women, just now, to see this. If they did so even now, after fifty years' discussion, the benumbing mental effect of political non-existence would be less demonstrated than it is.

The opposition to initiative is neither unprecedented nor inexplicable, nor of any special significance. Such opposition necessarily disappears with the necessity for initiative. We have never doubted the natural conservatism of women ; on the contrary, we have insisted upon it ; and the marvel is, that in the teeth of this immense conservative instinct and training, so many thousands of women do now demand the apparent innovation of the ballot. But similarly the Church, which fifty years ago was a unit in denouncing the public work of women— even for the slave,—is now divided in its counsels. If, in this Capitol of the State, the Church frowns on our claim, in the metropolis, in New York, this claim has received the eloquent and outspoken support of the clergy of all denominations, and few have openly opposed us.

The unequal feeling among women and their spiritual advisers in regard to the franchise, would have this effect —that enfranchisement, though sudden in its enactment, would be gradual in its operation. Enfranchisement is not a conscription, a draft. Voting is not compulsory upon men, nor has any one at present proposed to make it so. Evidently, therefore, it is absurd to imagine that the duty of the vote would be compulsory upon women.

which could be successfully challenged at the jury panel drawn to decide the pettiest wrong of the humblest citizen, cannot be that which is assumed, which is openly paraded by those to whom is committed the great rights of so many thousands, who are not the humblest. It is impossible that you should toss aside our claim, as the mere whim of a few irresponsible cranks, when already the petitions in its support number over 289,000 names. When were such petitions ever before presented in this Assembly Chamber? This is not a question like that of the Prohibition proposal, obviously unfit for place in a discussion on constitutional reform. Questions concerning the electorate belong here, and belong nowhere else, for they concern the fundamental organic law. Do not give to this question less thought than has been elsewhere bestowed upon proposals to extend the franchise. You are not obliged to thread the imbecile intricacies that clogged the English Reform Bills : in our more fortunate country, the problem may be worked out on broad and simple lines. And in seeking the suffrage for women, we do *not* propose to lower the franchise ; we are asking for lateral, not vertical extension ; we shall not even oppose such restrictions on the franchise as more extended experience may decide to be suitable ; we only demand that such restriction be placed on some other basis than that of sex.

This is a question for American men to settle with American women, and on American principles. We pray you, therefore, do not allow the issue to be confused by any foreign sentimentalism, by any mediæval and inherited prejudice, out of consonance with the well established social polity of this State.

We pray you, further, do not allow your decisions to be complicated by calculations of supposed party interest. This is not and cannot be a party question, for the women whom you may help to enfranchise, will belong to no separate party. Whatever the independence of their individual judgment on individual questions, and which is to be desired, their party affiliations will necessarily be those of their fathers, brothers, and husbands. They do not wish to enter political life pledged by ties of inconvenient gratitude to any one party. Rather, free from entangling alliances, they aim to secure the open-hearted and generous support of the best, the most far-sighted, the most patriotic among every party now represented in the State.

Finally, gentlemen, we are aware that with you does not rest the final responsibility of this great question. It is, indeed, a question too momentous to be decided by a body of two hundred men, however wise, and learned, and patriotic ; you do not assume to so decide it ; your mandate is not entrusted to you for that purpose.

Qualifications for the franchise, for the dignity of full citizenship, for a right to share in the Sovereignty, can only be decided by the whole people who are already Sovereign. Bring this question, we entreat you, before them ; let it be discussed for the next five months, not only in your councils, but throughout the length and breadth of the State—in its cities, its villages, its hamlets, its farms. Let it be discussed in families ; let the husband inquire of the wife, and the son of the mother, and the brother of the sister, how they would prefer the vote to be cast, whether for or against this amendment. Then only can be fully known the deliberate opinions, at this time, of the voters of the State, and of the women also. To submit this question to the people, does not irrevocably engage the responsibility of the Convention. To refuse to submit it, *is* to assume the responsibility of deciding the whole question without the vote of the people. We are aware that in 1867 this question was buried by an adverse Convention ; but we also remember that the people subsequently buried all the work of the entire Convention at the polls.

Should in November a popular vote be taken, then, whether the decision prove favorable, as in Wyoming and Colorado, or adverse, as in Rhode Island and South Dakota, we shall bow, as is inevitable, to the popular will ; we shall withdraw, and bide our time for another twenty years, when once more we, or our survivors or our successors, will present themselves before a new Constitutional Convention, to prefer—and then successfully—our claim.

M. P. J.